I0623100

TRAGIC INK

A HAVENWOOD FALLS NOVELLA

HEATHER HILDENBRAND

ABOUT THIS BOOK

All's fair in war and unrequited love.

Tattoo artist Gwen Facharro prefers working alone in her Havenwood Falls shop. Coworkers want to be friends, and friends ask too many questions. The last thing Gwen wants to do is answer them. Especially when her inked images tend to take on lives of their own—and not everyone uses the fae magic for good. If the Court finds out, she'll be tossed in jail. Or worse, banished from town forever.

Although they grew up together, Seelie warrior Rhys Graywalk has been very careful to keep Gwen at a distance. Between the secrets he keeps *for* her and the ones he keeps *from* her, his plate is already full. Romance isn't on the menu. It can't be. He has his orders.

But when the people around her start turning up dead, Gwen's fears become reality. Someone has discovered her secret. Someone who wants Gwen's talents for themselves. And they won't stop until they get it.

To separate the truth from the lies she's been told about her fae heritage, Gwen is forced to work with the only friend she's ever really known. She's just not sure she can handle rejection a second time.

HAVENWOOD FALLS BOOKS

More books releasing on a monthly basis

Also try the YA line, Havenwood Falls High

Stay up to date at www.HavenwoodFalls.com

ALSO BY HEATHER HILDENBRAND

Remembrance

Dirty Blood

Imitation

Bitter Rivalry

Whisper

On The Hunt for His Cougar

The Badge & The Bear

Wilde Bear

River Bear

Alpha Undercover

Guarded By The Alpha

A Risk Worth Taking

O Face

Austin & The Magical Jawbreaker

Copyright © 2018 Heather Hildenbrand, Ang'dora Productions, LLC

All rights reserved.

Published by

Ang'dora Productions, LLC

5621 Strand Blvd, Ste 210

Naples, FL 34110

Havenwood Falls and Ang'dora Productions and their associated logos are trademarks and/or registered trademarks of Ang'dora Productions, LLC.

Cover design by Regina Wamba at MaeIDesign.com

Except as permitted under the U.S. Copyright Act of 1976, no part of this publication may be reproduced, stored in a retrieval system, or transmitted in any form or by any means, electronic, mechanical, photocopying, recording, or otherwise, without written permission of the owner of this book.

Please do not participate in or encourage piracy of copyrighted materials in violation of the author's rights. Purchase only authorized editions.

This book is a work of fiction. Names, characters, and events are either products of the author's imagination or are used fictitiously, and any resemblance to actual persons, living or dead, is entirely coincidental.

CHAPTER 1

$\mathcal{T}$he buzz of the tattoo gun vibrated against my skin until the bone in my hand ached from holding it steady. This was my third tattoo of the night—and the longest by at least two hours. I hadn't stopped to stretch, and now my neck and shoulders were paying for it. The way I hung over my work, hovering and squinting to get it just right, left me stiff and aching. It was a pain in the ass, really, the soreness that would inevitably follow tomorrow morning. But I loved it. The concentration required for the precision of the lines. Bringing an art piece to life on the canvas of someone's skin. It was a thrill every time, even if this one was so large and time-consuming. We were on our third and final session, but at least the patient was compliant. Strangely silent, actually. But it was better than when they complained.

When I was finally finished with the bright blues of the seascape, and the aqua scales of the mermaid's tail had been shaded in to the edge of the fine lines, I switched off the machine and set it aside. On the table before me, Sean stirred and sighed as if he'd just woken from a peaceful slumber.

"Is that a wrap, then?" His Irish accent was still thick despite the fact that he'd lived in Havenwood Falls for as long as I could remember. And I'd grown up here.

I nodded my head. Only Sean could sleep through a full-color back piece. "That's it," I confirmed.

He sat up slowly, his large back and broad shoulders probably just as stiff as mine. If the numbness had worn off enough to let the pain set in, he didn't show it as he swung easily to his feet from the table where he'd spent the last few hours facedown. His graying hair was disheveled, but then my short blond hair probably looked about the same. My own shirt clung to my back where the stuffiness in the room had left me coated in sweat. It wasn't something I minded. Not when it was the result of giving someone a fresh piece. A shower did sound heavenly right about now, though.

Sean stood and stretched and then fell still again, waiting for what we both knew came next. Standing behind him, I slathered a thick layer of Vaseline over the mural I'd given him and then wrapped it in plastic. When I tried reminding him of the care instructions, he waved me off. "Yeah, yeah, I got it. This ain't my first rodeo, girl."

He was right. This was his fourteenth, if I was counting correctly.

I let it go and slid my gloves off while he shrugged into his button-down. He left the buttons open on the top half, revealing a hairy chest and the edges of the older ink that covered his shoulders and flowed down his arms.

"You're catching up to me," I told him with a raised brow.

"Nah. None of mine are worth even half of those." He nodded to the various tattoos flowing up and out of my black tank. My arms were covered down to my wrists, and my chest was inked up to the edges of my collarbone. The only tattoo that I hadn't done myself was a small symbol on my left shoulder. Magical in its own way, but not like the rest. If the Court of the Sun and the Moon, our local leaders, only knew their mark wasn't the only one on my body that held spells . . . Thankfully, they didn't. Yet.

Sean studied the hawk on my forearm with sharp eyes. Something like fear jangled my gut at the way his attention caught on it. His words finally sank in, and I stiffened.

"What do you mean?" I asked.

Sean blinked, but the gleam in his eye remained. And the certainty in his tone was unmistakable. "Come on. You know what I mean, Gwen. They say your tattoos are more than just ink."

Motherfucker.

Fourteen times this guy had been in my chair, and he'd never once let on he knew about me. About what I could do. If he had, I damn sure wouldn't have inked him. Partly out of principle. Mostly, to avoid this exact conversation.

"Look, Sean," I began. "I think you're mistaken about what it—"

"No mistake. But don't worry, your secret's safe." He looked believable enough, and I had known Sean for a long time now, but even so, my gut roiled with fear and the guilt that always gnawed at the edges. "Honestly, I've just been hoping you'd pour a bit of that magic of yours into some of the ink you've put on me. I'd never tell a soul if you did."

And there it was.

The request that only the really plugged-in residents of this town bothered to make. They wanted the magic. Too bad for them I wasn't giving it out anymore. Not unless I was forced, but that was another issue altogether. And if the first thirteen pieces I'd done for him were any indication, Sean should have known that already.

I narrowed my eyes. Maybe he was sent here to test me. Maybe Ada was checking to be sure she was still my only customer when it came to the top-tier services Tragic Ink could provide.

"Look, you got what you paid for. That's all I'm offering," I said in a tone that left no room for argument—or more questions.

He shrugged and backed off, heading for the door. "Sure, no problem. Next time," he said.

The way the words hung there, even after he'd left and the door had clicked shut behind him, made it hard to tell what he meant. Did he mean he'd see me next time? Or that he'd expect the bonus package next time?

I made a mental note not to tattoo Sean, the Irish healer, ever again.

Then, shoving aside my anxiety, I straightened the studio and shut everything down for the night. I checked my phone, which had been set to silent while I worked, and read the five texts from Aelwyn, my foster mother. The first three were reminders about what time she was expecting me. The last two were warnings not to be late again. I texted her back to let her know I was on my way, hoping I wouldn't have to hear a lecture about how tardiness was a form of disrespect—Aelwyn wasn't strict, but on this she'd always been a dog with a bone—and hauled ass while I cleaned up. Hurrying as I shut off the lights and the neon "Open" sign, I locked up and took off into the frigid night for Aelwyn's house.

The few residents that were out walking on Main Street never even noticed me as I slipped out the front door of my second-floor tattoo shop and down the stairs, taking a hard right into the alley that ran between my shop's building and the next. From there, I cut through the back alleyway that ran behind Eighth Street until I reached the narrow space where I parked my truck.

Sliding in, I fired it up and slid my palms together to warm them while I waited for the engine to heat to something warmer than the frigid temperature outside. Winter in the mountains of Colorado was not exactly tropical. To ward off the chill, I let some of my human glamour slip. In the shadows of my truck, I felt my ears lengthen and come to a point at the top and the shape of my face narrow.

My human glamour made me appear shorter than I was, so without it my head brushed the roof of the truck. My suddenly longer legs bent more sharply at the knees, too cramped for the seat, but I dealt with it just long enough to let the fae blood inside me heat my skin. Between that and the heating vents, it was enough.

I waited until my hands and toes had warmed. Then, just as quickly as I'd let it fall away, I called my glamour back up, and by the time I blinked, I looked human again. Blonde, slender, and covered in ink, though that last part never changed, glamour or not. The tattooed star tingled a bit as the magic it was laced with settled back into place. I'd had it since I was a kid, a requirement for all the permanent supernatural residents of Havenwood Falls. It was also the symbol that housed my glamour and logged me with the Court of the Sun and the Moon so they could keep track of who was supposed to be here—and who wasn't human. It also helped lessen my weakness to iron, which was a nice benefit considering the stuff was literally everywhere these days, and all fae were sensitive to it.

As I'd grown older, the fact that I'd chosen such a common symbol had irritated me, but I knew if I had to choose all over again, I would still pick it. The stars had always called to me, even as a little girl. In fact, when Ethan had sprung to life that first time, it had almost made sense to me that I'd conjured a creature with wings. My heart had always craved flight.

Almost as if he knew I was thinking of him, the gray hawk inked on my arm seemed to twitch impatiently. "Easy, boy," I muttered and shoved the truck into gear, rumbling out into the empty alley and from there to the outskirts of town.

The drive wasn't long, but it was just treacherous enough this time of year to slow me down even more.

Aelwyn had always been supportive of my tattoo business. She'd been the one to encourage my art and to help me discover what sort of magic I was capable of using with it. She'd also been there to see Ethan come to life. And because of her support, I knew, once a week, she willingly ate dinner late just so we could have this time together after my work was finished. Still, keeping her waiting was a good way to be greeted with a lecture. I wanted to avoid that part if possible. A hot meal settled better when it wasn't preceded by a tongue-lashing.

My stomach twisted as I wondered if I would be the only dinner guest. Just as quickly as I thought it, I shoved it away. He hadn't been there in months, thanks to the bar he'd bought last year taking up so much time. And even when he did show, we barely spoke. It had been like that for years now. What was one more awkward dinner?

Nothing, I told myself. It was nothing. *He* was nothing.

It was utterly dark when I parked in front of the old Victorian where I'd grown up. Trees surrounded it, with only the winding drive ribboning in from the mountain road providing a view of the place. My headlights cast a narrow beam over the front entry, and I frowned as I pulled to a stop directly in front rather than off to the side where I usually parked. Something wasn't right. Trying to figure it out, I looked around to check the solar-powered lanterns that led the way across the lawn to the front door. None of them were lit. The porch light wasn't either. I looked closer and frowned. Even the lights inside were off.

Something anxious curled in my gut.

I left my headlights on and the engine running as I got out. Taking care to keep to the shadows, I crept around the shrubs as the gray hawk on my arm stirred and scratched. This time, I didn't hold back. The darkness would shield any prying eyes, and besides, I might need him. Despite the cold, I peeled my jacket away, revealing my tank top and bare arm underneath.

With silent permission, I let the magic call him forth. On a sigh, he raised his beak, already on alert, and in the next blink, the hawk had peeled itself away from my skin, its body filling in with form and feathers until it was much more than the ink outline I'd drawn on myself years ago.

With a sharp keening sound, my familiar took to the skies, soaring up and over the rooftop, doing a quick loop to investigate. I slid my jacket back into place and took a shallow breath, my eyes half-closed as I concentrated on the magic that allowed me to see the world through Ethan's eyes. I rarely allowed him loose like this so close to town where humans might see, but the darkness and the slithering unease that raced up my spine left me too anxious to resist.

When Ethan had done a full loop and found nothing out of the ordinary, I blinked, clearing my sight and refocusing on the yard in front of me. Slowly, with a silent stealth inherent to fae, I crept toward the front door.

I tried glancing in through the darkened window as I passed. Nothing moved inside.

My heart beat faster.

Aelwyn had been old when I'd been brought to her as a baby. Even by fae standards, which was saying something, because of how slowly we aged compared to humans. If she'd lost her balance and fallen . . .

But that still didn't explain the dark house.

With a steadying breath, I tried the knob, twisting it in my hand and shoving inside. The hinges creaked, and I waited, listening. The scent of mistletoe hit me first. Not unusual. Aelwyn had an affinity for the stuff, and her garden out back was covered in it. But something was off. I just didn't know what.

Somewhere in the back of the house, there was the tiniest creak of a floorboard.

I flew into motion.

Racing for the kitchen, I tore down the narrow hall, skipping the living and dining rooms as I passed them on my right and left. It was dark as hell, but I knew my way around this house, lights or no.

When I reached the kitchen, I flipped the switch and was a little surprised to see the overhead light come on so easily. It washed the room in a yellowish tone, and I blinked at the sudden change. The back door stood wide open, the yawning darkness of the backyard beckoning me. I almost obeyed, but something out of the corner of my eye stopped me.

I whirled, searching.

A pot stood simmering on the stove, red sauce bubbling up the sides. Another pot sat in the sink. Spaghetti. She'd been making my favorite. When I caught sight of a chunk of white hair peeking out from behind the stove, I closed the distance, curving around the pantry and pulling up short.

My lips parted, but no sound came.

I dropped to my knees.

My mother lay on the floor, her legs curled at an awkward angle. Her white hair was splayed around her face, fanning out around her so that the ends were mixing with the pool of blood that was leaking fast from her abdomen and chest onto the floor underneath her.

"Ma," I choked out, my hands hovering over her uncertainly.

All I wanted to do was help her. But I had no idea how.

At the sound of my voice, her lids fluttered and then her blue eyes opened, squinting as if in pain. They widened when she saw me. "Gwenllian."

"What happened?" My voice cracked as I struggled to hold back a sob. "What can I do?"

"Nothing. It is too late to help me." She pressed her lips together, and her face contorted sharply.

A sob escaped. "Ma, please. You can't—"

I broke off, unable to say the word.

Die. She couldn't die. Not yet. Not like this.

"Listen to me now," she said quietly. "Hush and listen. I have kept this from you solely for your own safety. I thought I would have more time, but . . ."

"More time for what?" I asked through tears that blurred her face until I could barely make her out.

She drew a slow, pained breath. I squeezed her hand, willing her to go on. Part of me wanted to tell her to save her breath. To hang on while I ran for help. But something held me there. Something that knew these were our last moments, and I wasn't willing to waste them on pointless efforts. I blinked until I could see her weathered cheeks and light eyes once more.

"Gwen, you are special. Important. I've done all I can, but they have never stopped hunting you. You must not let them find you. Leave this house. Don't come back. Find Rhys. He will know what to do."

"What are you talking about, Aelwyn? Who is hunting me? Who did this to you?" Her words jumbled against each other in my mind—all of them taking a backseat to the puddle of blood I was now sitting in, while still more leaked from the fresh wounds on her chest. The horror of watching her bleed out this way overrode any sense I might have made of whatever secrets she was trying to spill.

She clutched my hand much too weakly, her eyes pleading with mine. "You are a bright star, Gwenllian. Much too bright to conceal. But you can't hide anymore. They have come for you. And you must not run from that. You must not run from who you are."

"I don't understand what you're saying," I sobbed. "Who am I hiding from?"

Aelwyn didn't answer, and for a terrifying moment, I thought she was already gone. My head bowed, and I leaned in to lay my head on her shoulder, my cries filling the silence.

"You will," she whispered, so low I might have missed it if I hadn't been lying so close to her lips. "Rhys will protect you. He always has."

"Rhys?" I sat up, confused and heartsick at the thought of asking him for anything.

"Promise me," she said, because Aelwyn knew. She'd always known. Somehow. "Please."

"I promise," I said, my voice breaking. My heart ached, because it was a promise I would keep no matter how much I didn't want to. The first stirrings of rage began in my gut. Even now, I could see the life fading in her, and I knew that when she was gone, I would have nothing else stopping me from my revenge. "Now tell me who did this."

"I love you, *nighean*."

Daughter.

It was what she called me when she was trying to comfort or reassure me, usually when my magic had gone awry or my heart had felt broken. And it was absolutely broken now. "I love you too, Ma. Don't go."

She didn't answer.

My shoulders shook as I lay with my cheek against her shoulder and my hand still squeezing hers. A coldness had seeped into her skin, and now, it felt odd, like I was holding onto a stranger. Thinking that only made me cry harder.

Outside, Ethan gave a sharp call, and I jerked my head up, blinking away the tears that blurred the kitchen cabinets as I looked toward the open door. For a split second, it all slid into place. The reality hit me that Aelwyn was gone and someone had taken her from me. And that someone might still be close by. For a moment, that was enough to dull the grief and sharpen my thoughts.

I looked down at Aelwyn. Her blue eyes were closed, and her chest no longer moved with the rise and fall of labored breaths. I swallowed back a scream as I searched for a pulse. I found none.

And just like that, my helplessness vanished. Instead, I had purpose. Not once in my life had I chosen violence to solve something. In fact, the only time violence had occurred at my hands, I'd spent the next few years punishing myself for it. But now, tonight, violence called to me. The idea of avenging Aelwyn made my blood sing.

No longer frozen in shock, I rose slowly to my feet. When I heard Ethan call again, I sucked in a breath and twisted toward the door. It was a battle cry. The call he used to let me know when he'd found his prey. Sometimes, when I loosed him in the woods behind the house, we'd hunt together. Him with his talons and sharp eyes as he soared overhead. Me with the bow and quiver I kept in my old room upstairs. Tonight, though, I had a feeling he wasn't signaling dinner.

I wiped my bloody palms on my dark jeans and ran to the knife block, yanking free the largest of the blades. I clutched it tight in my stained hand before racing out into the darkness in the direction of Ethan's call. If Aelwyn's murderer was still out there, I was going to find them. And when I did, I was going to kill them.

CHAPTER 2

*T*he backyard was small, bordered on all sides by woods. The trees were broken up by narrow walking paths I used to skip down as a kid. Tonight, the paths were lit by the moon's glow reflecting off the snow covering the ground. I used the light and Ethan's sharp cries to direct me as I ran.

Trees flew by as I sprinted, and branches scraped along my face and tangled in my hair. I would have kept going, too, lungs screaming, legs aching, but in the end, my chase only led me in a large loop. Eventually, I spilled out of the trees back where I'd started—and ran right into a broad chest.

"Ommph." I tried jumping backward, terrified I'd just thrown myself into the arms of a killer, but hands came up to squeeze my arms and held me still.

"Whoa, there. It's just me." The voice was masculine and rich, and I hated the sound the instant it invaded my head. As if I hadn't tortured myself enough with the memory of him on the drive over. Or every waking moment, if I was being honest. Now he was here, his presence mingling with my panic. And I hated how badly I wanted to let him save me.

"Let me go," I demanded, silently calling for Ethan to come and swoop down on my assaulter. The traitor remained airborne and silent.

"Gwen? Are you all right?" The voice came again, and I dragged my gaze upward, past a thick winter coat and shirt that I knew hid solid abs and broad shoulders, still struggling against the iron grip he had on me. But when I caught sight of that familiar set of dark eyes, I shivered at the rush of longing that always threatened to overwhelm me when I saw him.

"Aelwyn . . ." My bottom lip trembled, and before I could stop it, a sob escaped my throat. Desperate and panicked and at a loss for what to do next, I came apart, with tears and more sobs following quickly behind the first.

"I know." Strong arms came around me, pulling me close, and I clung to him, ashamed of my vulnerable display, but too embarrassed to pull away and let him see my tear-stained face. Not to mention the snot I knew was close behind if I didn't get my shit together pronto.

But every time I tried to take a deep breath, more tears leaked out and my shoulders only shook harder. Quiet murmurs comforted me, and a gloved hand ran over my neck and back, sending tingles down my spine. His flannel smelled like spilled whiskey and cigarette smoke—and him. There was nothing else in the world that smelled like him. Still, it wasn't worth this. Because I knew there would be no coming back from the mortification of crying in his arms.

After what had happened inside with Aelwyn and now this, tonight couldn't have been more of a nightmare. Even so, my heart thudded wildly in my chest at the feel of his arms around me. The truth was Rhys Graywalk hadn't been in nearly as many of my nightmares as he had my dreams. For that, I hated him.

With that thought in mind, grief and embarrassment turned quickly to rage. But I forced even that aside and somehow managed to conjure something resembling stony indifference. I sniffled one last time, used my jacket sleeve to swipe at my eyes and nose, and then stepped back, eyes downcast.

Overhead, Ethan circled, and I could feel his urge to return to me, but I willed him away with a command that probably came out rude rather than urgent. I wasn't in the mood to return him to my arm. Not with Rhys watching. He didn't get to know my secrets. Not anymore.

"What are you doing here?" I asked, my voice choked with the effort of trying to sound casual after all the snot I'd just left on his shirt.

"I came for dinner and then I saw—" He stopped, and I was glad he didn't finish that sentence. "Gwen," he said again, this time much softer. "Are you all right?"

"I'm fine. It's Ma. She—"

"I know." He wouldn't let me finish, and for that I was legitimately grateful. No part of me wanted to describe what I'd seen in the kitchen.

"She was . . . still alive when I got here," I said, my voice small. I steeled myself and looked up, meeting his eyes. I ignored the concern he gave off. My hands balled into fists, partly from the cold that was finally starting to settle in and partly to keep away the butterflies that batted my rib cage. I hated to look at him. No, that was a lie. I hated to look when he was watching.

"Did she say who did it?" he asked, his words hopeful enough that I felt bad when I shook my head.

"No. She said some other stuff, though." I frowned. "About you. And about me . . . being special—whatever that means. It didn't make a lot of sense."

He nodded, not at all surprised, like I expected he would be. "We can talk about all of that. Come on. The sheriff's on his way. And it's cold as shit out here."

I didn't question Rhys. Not about warming up inside—although I wasn't sure I wanted to wait in the kitchen. And not about offering to help me decipher Aelwyn's last words. Whatever he'd been or done to me, Rhys had always looked out for us ever since we were kids. Three years older than me, he'd come to Aelwyn when he was ten. She'd taken him in without question, just as she'd done for me years earlier. And from the day he arrived, Rhys had been everything to both of us. A friend and playmate for me. A handyman for Aelwyn. He'd moved out at eighteen, but even after things had fallen apart between us, he'd still taken care of her. I was grateful for that. But he didn't need to know it.

My heart thundered in my chest as I let Rhys lead the way into the house. When he stopped to hold the back door for me, my arm brushed his shirt as I passed, and my insides curled in traitorous enjoyment. Even now, in the middle of this nightmare, my body reacted to him on a chemical level I'd never been able to escape.

The lights were on now. Not just the kitchen, but the hall and a few lamps in the living and dining rooms as well. The pot on the stove had been moved and the burner turned off. Rhys, I assumed. I didn't bother to ask. Instead, I returned hesitantly to where Aelwyn lay on the floor. The pooled blood was larger than before, but her wounds no longer leaked with it. Her eyes were closed, and she might have looked peaceful even, if not for the blood and the wounds. I dropped to the floor beside her, my eyes filling with tears.

Rhys didn't speak, nor did he try to force me away, and I sat there, unmoving, until I heard the crunch of tires over the yard as a car pulled up. Doors opened, then closed. I did my best to quiet my own crying and sniffled hard as someone rapped on the front door. Footsteps behind me shuffled out and down the hall. I stayed where I was, listening as Rhys spoke quietly to the sheriff.

"You found her like that?" the sheriff asked when Rhys explained what they were about to walk in on.

"Yes. She was already dead when I got here," he said, and I flinched at the word. Dead. Yes, she'd already been dead. Because someone had killed her. And I'd let them get away.

"Did you call her other foster child? Gwen?" the sheriff asked.

"She's here," Rhys told him, and there was a beat of silence.

"Show me."

I waited while heavy boots made their way toward me. With a last swipe at my eyes, I looked up as they entered. Rhys came in first and crossed to stand beside me. The sheriff, a broad-shouldered werewolf with a permanent scowl, frowned when he caught sight of me kneeling over Aelwyn's body.

"Miss Facharro," the sheriff said, his expression grumpy.

"Sheriff," I said quietly.

But his eyes were on Rhys, and he looked pissed. "You let her touch the body?"

"She got here first. Damage was already done."

The sheriff huffed. A beat of silence passed. He stood stiffly with one hand propped on his weapon, and I watched that hand very carefully as he stared back at me. Distrust rolled off him. Nothing new there. No law enforcement official in this town trusted me. Not after—

"I'm going to need you to step away from the bod—from your mother." Sheriff Kasun moved aside, and I finally saw the second officer. Conall, Kasun's son, although younger and slightly shorter, was a carbon copy of his father, permanent scowl included. "This is Deputy Conall. You can give him your statement while I conduct an investigation of the scene."

I didn't answer. Instead, I turned back to my mother and leaned close, pressing a kiss to her cheek before climbing slowly to my feet. Rhys held out his hand, but I ignored him. I couldn't risk touching him in front of watchful eyes. Not when I knew my body would react so obviously.

When I was upright, I fastened the deputy with a look that I hoped made him wonder if I really was capable of whatever rumors he'd heard. I didn't know what those rumors might have been, and I didn't care. But if he was nervous about me, maybe that would motivate him to resolve this quickly. Behind me, Rhys shifted his weight, and I got the sense he was amused more than impatient. Still, I held the deputy's uncertain stare. The sheriff cleared his throat, and the deputy blinked, ending our standoff.

"Right. We can just go into the living room," he muttered, turning on his heel and leading the way.

I followed and was secretly glad when Rhys stayed behind.

In the living room, the deputy took one of the armchairs. I suspected it was a trick to get me to sit, too, but I remained on my feet. Too wired. Too on edge. My thoughts flicked to Ethan somewhere outside, and I frowned. My jacket covered the empty place on my arm, but I was antsy to get him put away again.

"Miss Facharro," he began, whipping a pad and pen out of his belt loop. "Why don't you tell me what happened. Start at the beginning."

So I did.

In a low voice that only shook when I came to the part about discovering my mother bleeding on the floor, I told him everything that had happened. When I'd finished, he was frowning. "You heard a noise, and instead of calling the police, you went racing after it into the dark woods?"

"Of course," I said. "If I'd waited for you guys, he would have definitely gotten away."

"He?" His brow rose. "So it was a male?"

"I . . . Well, I can't be sure, as I didn't see anyone, but I get a sense that . . . it was." Actually, it was Ethan who'd gotten that sense, but I couldn't exactly share the findings from my magical hawk or the fact that I had a familiar thanks to a magical tattoo that the Court of the Sun and the Moon currently knew nothing about.

"A sense," the deputy repeated in a tone that made me want to tattoo a thousand mosquitos on my skin and aim them all at him.

"That's right," I said through clenched teeth.

I braced myself, waiting for him to mock me outright. Instead, he said, "And can you think of anyone that might have wanted to hurt your foster mother?"

"My mother," I said.

"Excuse me?"

"She might have been a foster mother on paper, but she was a mom to me. The best mom anyone could ask for."

"Right. Of course. Your mother," he corrected. "Who might have wanted to hurt her?"

"No one," I said honestly. "She didn't have any enemies."

I waited while he wrote something down. When he was finished, he closed his pad and stood, sliding both pad and pen back into his belt loop.

"Thank you for your time," he said, and then walked out.

I stayed where I was, listening while he returned to the kitchen and assisted the sheriff in collecting evidence. Both of them moved slow as hell, and it was another hour before the coroner and an official evidence team even showed up.

By then, any expectations I'd had about the police actually giving a shit or doing anything productive here tonight to catch a killer had disappeared.

I STOOD ALONE in the dining room until a noise behind me made me turn. Rhys leaned against the doorframe, watching me.

"What?" I asked, but it lacked venom. I was exhausted, and the grief was starting to cloud out the shock that had been fueling me until now. I considered taking a shot from the espresso tattooed on my left forearm, but I didn't want to risk being seen. All I wanted was solitude—so I could fall apart.

"They'll find who did this," he said.

I turned back to the window, watching as a two-man crew loaded my mother's body into the back of a transport vehicle bound for the medical examiner's office in town.

"How?" I asked finally.

Rhys took a step forward.

I turned to glare at him, my face already hot with the words on my

15

tongue. "How in the hell will they find her killer? They have no leads, and they didn't even send someone out to check the perimeter of the property?"

"Sheriff Kasun promised me he already has a team on it," he said.

"Whatever," I muttered. So far, Ethan hadn't been impressed by the wolves he'd seen investigating the property line.

"Gwen—"

"They don't believe me that someone was out there."

He took another step. "I do."

I looked away, back to the window where I saw the paramedics finishing up. The doors were closing now. The engines were turning over. This was it. After tonight, I would never see my mother again. This house would never feel the same. An irrational panic rose, clogging the back of my throat. A part of me wanted to fling open the front door and race out there to stop them. To keep my mother—or what was left of her—here. Even if it didn't make sense.

I forced my feet to remain where they were. "You believe me," I said dully. "What good does that do me?"

"A lot, if you'll let me help."

I turned to study him, unwilling to watch my mother be carted away from the only home I'd ever known with her. Instead, I put all of my attention and focus on the words Rhys had just spoken. And the ones he hadn't said out loud.

"Help with what?" I asked, wary and curious as I remembered Aelwyn's last words. The promise I'd made rang in my ears. I couldn't go back on that, but damn it, I couldn't ask Rhys for anything.

"We both know what," he said and then snorted. "The only mother either of us has ever known was murdered," he went on, and I flinched but didn't contradict him. Better to face the truth, no matter how hard, than live in denial. "And I know you're not going to rest until you figure out who killed her. I think you know that I won't either. And I can help you. If you let me."

"I thought that's what the police are for," I challenged.

Rhys sighed. "I heard Kasun speculating it could be related to the Bennett girl's disappearance last year."

"It could," I argued, with no real idea why I was suddenly sticking up for that asshat—except that I didn't want to side with Rhys.

He pinned me with a look, and in the dim lamplight, his eyes flashed. "You don't believe that for a second. Neither do I."

"I don't know—"

"Those woods—out there where I found you earlier—have traces of fae all over them, but it's unreadable. I've never seen anything like it. It's just . . . a ghost. The only real signature that's even remotely detectable out there is yours. Whoever was here used a glamour to cover his tracks."

That silenced me. I thought it had just been me. My own signature. Or Ethan was losing his touch, but . . .

"Does the sheriff know that?" I asked quietly.

"Yes."

"Does he also know that Aelwyn didn't let fae come to the house?" I asked, a strange sort of uncertainty sending a tingling down my spine. It had been a strange thing, Aelwyn's rule. She'd never explained it either, but it had been ironclad. No fae on her land. Period. If I hadn't known her so well, I'd have wondered if she was prejudiced or maybe bitter about something in her past, but she'd been friendly enough with everyone in town, fae included.

I'd never really thought about how strange her rule was until now. Or her unyielding routine of warding the house with fresh herbs and magic every month on the full moon.

Rhys didn't question it either, though, which only made it all the weirder. "I told him, but . . ."

He trailed off, and I caught his expression before he shifted away. Concerned. Hesitant. It set a warning bell off in my head, and I bit my lip as the pieces fell together. The police weren't very fond of me, thanks to a childhood spent as a loner and, on occasion, as a troublemaker. I'd broken into a building in high school and set up shop, using it as a temporary tattoo parlor. I'd made a few thousand dollars before they'd shut me down. I'd also made enemies out of Havenwood Falls' finest.

Apparently, they held a grudge.

I braced myself and asked quietly, "Am I a suspect?"

The beat of silence that followed told me all I needed to know. "Not officially."

I cursed. A long string of them that would have gotten my mouth washed with soap had I been younger. Aelwyn would have lectured me even now if she'd been here. And suddenly, the emptiness of the house washed over me. I had to get out.

"I have to go," I said, shoving past Rhys and crossing to the front door. I yanked it open, relieved now to see everyone else had gone, and strode out into the night. Overhead, Ethan circled. *Just a few more minutes.* I'd have to make a pit stop on the way home so I could put him away before I got back to town.

My truck was still where I'd parked it, but halfway there, I realized the headlights were off. They'd been on when I'd jumped out earlier. Before I could speculate why or who, Rhys was there, holding my keys out.

"I didn't want your battery to die," he explained.

"Thanks," I muttered, swiping the keys from him and heading for the truck.

"Aren't you forgetting something?"

I paused, one leg already in the truck. "What?"

Rhys pointed to the sky at the same time Ethan did a low loop overhead. I swallowed hard, debating whether to deny it. But what was the point anymore?

I sighed. "How did you know?"

"You shouldn't leave him loose for too long. Too many risks in this part of the woods," he said, ignoring my question.

I strode up to him until we were nose to nose in the darkness. Or nose to chin, since he was taller than me.

"How did you know?" I repeated. The temper that rolled off me was a welcome distraction to the grief building in my chest.

His eyes flashed with a knowing that rocked me. It was a look that suggested he knew a lot more about me than I might think. More than I ever told him, that was for sure. And I wondered if maybe my soul was the traitor, opening for him so willingly when he looked at me that way, so that he could just read it all for himself somehow. Like my heart just willingly gave up whatever he wanted from it.

I felt caught by his gaze, like a deer caught by oncoming headlights. One hundred percent of me was certain this was going to end with me wrecked.

"Let me help you, Gwen," he said softly.

His words were enough to break the spell.

I blinked, shaking my head to clear the fog that made it hard to remember why I didn't want his help in the first place. But the moment I remembered, my jaw hardened, and I stepped back, no longer trusting myself to stand so close to him.

"Aelwyn might have tied us together, but that common bond is gone now. Go home, Rhys. And leave me alone. For good this time."

I couldn't help the sadness that laced my words, but I told myself it was exhaustion and the loss I'd suffered tonight. Rhys didn't argue, and he didn't call out to me as I trudged back to my truck. I slid inside and turned the engine over, gunning it out of the yard and onto the main road. Just before the trees obscured my view, I glanced into my rearview. But the darkness was complete, and I saw nothing but shadows of the past in my wake.

CHAPTER 3

*E*than had whined all night and into the morning, and I knew my own tears probably had a lot to do with his distress. Rhys hadn't tried calling, though he'd texted that I should call him about making arrangements when I was ready. I wasn't sure whether to be glad or disappointed that he hadn't tried to come by. I'd made my wishes clear with him, but still. He was the only person in the world who knew Aelwyn. And me. The real me. The temptation to let him comfort me was strong—until I remembered what that would cost me in the end. Better not to go down that road.

Unfortunately, that left me no one else. In fact, when it came to the rest of the world, I wanted to hide. But there was nowhere in the world that I could go where Aelwyn was still alive. Not to mention anywhere I wasn't a murder suspect. But I was determined not to think about that until I absolutely had to. So, the next afternoon, when I'd tossed and turned and then showered until the hot water ran cold, I descended the stairs from my third-floor apartment to my second-floor shop, Tragic Ink, and opened for business.

Twenty minutes later, I wished I hadn't.

The chime sounded, signaling the door opening, and I rounded the corner while schooling my features into something that didn't resemble a grief-stricken zombie. When I saw who it was, my blood turned cold, and I stopped in my tracks. This was not what I'd had in mind when I'd intended to let work distract me from my grief.

"Hello, Gwen." A middle-aged woman waltzed in, her smile genuinely evil, calculating, and completely sure of herself as she rounded the counter with a thickly muscled man in tow.

"What do you want, Ada?" I asked, my eyes narrowing in disgust and wariness. Ethan scratched at my arm, but my own will kept him from making any real noise.

The man glanced up at me and then away again as he followed her around the corner and sat where she directed him. No question who was in charge here.

"You know what I want," she said so matter-of-factly, it was almost easy to miss the sharp edge to her tone. Almost.

But Ada wasn't someone I could afford to underestimate. Ada was the leader of the Green Coven, a group of witches suspected of practicing black magic. The Court of the Sun and the Moon overlooked Ada's methods for one reason only: because she would get her hands dirty when they wouldn't. No real accusations had ever been made, but I suspected that was all part of the backdoor dealings she had going on already—if the Court banished her, the town would lose one of their best hit men.

A quick-tempered witch with zero respect for the law, Ada Daryn was the worst of Havenwood Falls. So I didn't miss the way she always sugar-coated things when she was trying to hide her temper. Or the way her mood could shift on a dime.

A thousand times, I'd convinced myself to stand up to her. I'd even designed tattoos that might help me fight her off when she realized I wasn't going to do her bidding. But Ada wasn't someone to mess with. She was, however, in a position to mess with me. So in the end, I always gave in and did the work. I just hated myself for it later.

Tonight, though, my emotions were so frayed already, I wasn't sure I could deal with Ada and her shit.

"Tonight's not a good night," I said, willing to appeal to her compassion, if she had any.

Her eyes narrowed and then gleamed at my words, and I knew then the term *compassion* didn't exist in her vocabulary.

"Really?" She clucked her tongue. "That's unfortunate. I guess I could come back later. That would give me plenty of time to activate all the magic you've already inked for me. And when the police get those calls of mayhem and chaos unleashed on their lovely town, the only explanation I could give would be to admit where I'd gotten the magic from. Of course, that would mean you aren't available another night either. Not in this lifetime anyway."

"I'm not in the mood to be threatened, either," I warned, her words only serving to piss me off further. Maybe tonight was the night I'd finally tell her no.

But Ada's eyes sharpened, and she didn't look nearly as nervous at my rejection as I thought she would. "I would have thought you'd be a little more interested in self-preservation than this. What with last night's incident."

I went still. "What does Aelwyn have to do with any of this?"

Ada blinked. "Aelwyn?" She waved a hand. "Nothing at all. The mountain lion at the Village Apartments is something I assumed you'd be concerned about."

"Why the hell would I be concerned about that?" I tried to think back, but I'd been so caught up in getting to Aelwyn's last night. And then when I'd come home . . . I hadn't exactly sat down and watched the news.

"Because when it was done ransacking a first-floor apartment, it just vanished. Poof." She snapped her fingers, and I flinched. "Just like that. Strange, right?"

I pressed my lips together and tried to resist the urge to lift my shirt and check my own skin for the mountain lion I wore. Ada stood, waiting smugly, and I knew I had to call her bluff. If she was right and my tattoo had come to life—again—I was screwed.

Heart pounding, I turned away from her and the man who had sat patiently through all this, and lifted my shirt a few inches. I peered down at the collage of ink on my skin, searching. When my eyes landed on the spot where the mountain lion had been, I went still. A tiny patch of blank skin stared back at me, surrounded by the other images still sitting dormant on me—carbon copies of the magical tattoos I'd given out to others.

They all sat ready and waiting on my body until the magic was triggered. Then, they sprang to life just as the original was called to action by its wearer. The first time it had happened, I'd followed my own ink and arrived just in time to witness the chaos it caused. This time, I'd completely missed it. My grief had wiped me out last night, and when I'd finally passed out, apparently I'd slept hard.

Damn it. Ada was right. That mountain lion was my fault.

My gut twisted as I turned back to Ada. "Was anyone hurt?"

"No, the police were able to rescue the woman inside. Her ex-boyfriend was caught trying to flee the scene, however, and one eyewitness swears the boyfriend somehow conjured the mountain lion out of thin air. Quite a feat for a prairie dog shifter with no magic beyond his own shifting ability."

"Was he arrested?" I asked, trying to ignore the brick forming in my stomach, because I knew exactly which customer she referred to.

I'd given him the mountain lion a year and a half ago because he'd cried in my shop about how lame it was being a prairie dog shifter. Just once, he'd wanted to experience what it would be like as a predator and not prey. The mountain lion was supposed to be just for him. For a night of fun alone in the woods. Not to terrorize his ex-girlfriend.

"As a matter of fact, he's been called in for questioning," Ada said. "Conall, I think, was the officer on the scene. Isn't he the one investigating Aelwyn's murder? Small town, I guess." She smiled softly, and my shoulders slumped.

She had me.

"What do you want me to do?" I asked quietly.

"Nothing difficult." She beamed. "This one will be quick and easy for you."

"And in exchange, you'll make sure the mountain lion doesn't lead here?" I asked.

"Of course. You scratch my back, I scratch yours." Ada smirked at me.

I tried not to throw up. Ada still hadn't told me why she didn't just do these tattoos herself. She was much more powerful than me, and I was sure she could have figured it out, but she still came here. I suspected she just didn't want her own magic signature on them, but I wasn't sure why she'd even care. She got away with everything else.

Moving on autopilot, I went to retrieve my tools, and when I turned to face them again, the man had removed his shirt. He'd turned in the chair so that his back was exposed, and I winced at all the hair coating his skin. Werewolf, probably. Or bear shifter. And I didn't recognize him, which meant he was either new or a loner. Ada had probably chosen him to carry out some horrible deed for her. I tried not to imagine what that might be. Ada never told me what she intended with the tattoos she forced me to do for her minions, and I hadn't asked. If this ever came back on me, it was one less conspiracy charge. Or that's what I told myself.

"What'll it be?" I asked, wishing again that I'd just stayed in bed. Even calling Rhys back to discuss funeral arrangements sounded better than this.

"He needs an asp wrapped around his right bicep."

"An asp?" I blinked at her.

"Yes, it's a venomous snake that—"

"I know what it is." I felt the horror transform my features. "You can't be serious."

Her lips curved. "*Dead* serious."

"Ada, that's . . . I can't." In the pit of my stomach was an absolute certainty that this tattoo would bring someone harm. No part of me wanted to cause that ever again.

"You can and you will, or I'll tell the Court what you did. What you're capable of. Whom you've hurt with your *art*." The last word dripped with sarcasm.

"It was an accident," I said, but that didn't matter. Not to Ada. Not to the Court. And not to me. She was right. I'd hurt that woman. Didn't matter that her husband had housed the weapon. I'd been the one to ink him with it. I'd given him the loaded gun. He'd just pulled the trigger. "I can't let it happen again."

Ada rolled her eyes. "Your altruistic intentions will hardly matter to the Court," she snapped. "Your cursed tattoo took a woman's life, and that is all they will care about. You'll spend the rest of your life in a cell. And in the end, you will not have stopped me. With or without your tattoo, I will accomplish what I'm after."

She was right. About all of it.

But I still had one more card to play.

"Tell me about my mother's investigation," I said, levelling my gaze on hers and holding it steady even though my insides trembled. I'd never demanded anything of her before, and I wasn't entirely convinced it was the smart play now. But asking nicely wouldn't get me anywhere either.

"An ongoing investigation is classified." Ada scoffed. "How would I know anything about—"

"Classified information is your favorite kind, and we both know it. Besides, you have your snaky fingers in every pie this town has to offer. So I know you know something. Tell me what leads they have on Aelwyn's killer, and I'll do the tattoo."

Ada glared at me, and I wondered for a moment if she was capable of killing me with just her eyes. But finally, she blinked, and her lips curved upward in a sneer. "Why, I thought you knew," she said, too sweet. Too accommodating.

"Knew what?"

"The only suspect they have is you."

CHAPTER 4

The moment Ada was gone, I closed the shop and went upstairs. With all of the lights still burning, I shed my clothes and climbed into bed, careful to keep my bow and arrows close. Aelwyn had taught me to use them in our backyard as a kid. Since then, it had been a fun hobby that helped explain the long periods I spent in the woods with Ethan. But tonight, it was a comfort. Not that I anticipated a need for self-defense, but my impromptu appointments with Ada always left me on edge. Her special requests were awful and draining, but this one had been worse. Coming to me when I was already off-balance and requesting a tattoo that was obviously meant to harm twisted my stomach in knots.

The new tattoo itched. I lifted my sleeve to scratch it and frowned when I caught sight of the snake's tongue where it blended with a vine of orchids that had already been there from another one I'd given out a few years back. My magical tattoos just sort of showed up on my skin. I didn't get to place them. They appeared in the same spot I'd inked them on the client. As a result, I had a collage of two or sometimes four or five tattoos overlaid, thanks to the fact that most people chose the same spot on their bodies for new ink. They also itched as if I'd actually inked them on my own skin, which was completely unfair in my opinion. Regardless, my upper arms, shoulder blades, and calves were covered. Some of them were so blended with past images, they were unrecognizable. I really wished that had been the case with the snake. Sadly, it was easy to spot among the orchids.

On my other arm, Ethan was still mostly unhindered, but I suspected that was because he somehow shoved aside anything that encroached on his territory. He'd been the first enchanted image I'd given myself when my gifts had developed, and it still thrilled me to know I'd created at least one creature that wasn't used for nefarious purposes. He was also the only enchantment on my body that was permanent. Mostly because I was too scared of getting caught to create more.

Aelwyn speculated that all of my own self-induced ink would always be that way: magical and permanent. The magic I gifted to others expired once they'd used it up. Thank goodness for that. People were so mean. It was the reason I stayed away from them. After witnessing the destruction my tattoos could cause, I hadn't given myself or anyone else a magical tattoo in a long time. Except for Ada's minions, of course. I hated her for those.

I lay in bed and thought of Rhys's offer to help me figure out who had murdered Aelwyn. Not to mention the fact that his senses had picked up on a strange fae behind the house. I couldn't believe the sheriff hadn't sensed that, but considering me as a suspect was insane. Sure, the cops didn't like me, but a murder suspect? It was beyond ridiculous.

With Aelwyn gone, Rhys was officially the only person in the entire world who was on my side.

He was also the one person in the world who could hurt me deeply. Who already had. And I wasn't sure I had the strength to survive it again. Not now. So I'd wait. See what I could uncover on my own. And hope the killer didn't strike again in the meantime. Or leave a trail that led back to me.

The problem was Aelwyn didn't have a single enemy in the world. Who would have wanted to hurt her? That question stumped me and, in the end, left me in tears as I tried to imagine moving forward without her wisdom, or her worry constantly hanging over me.

Ethan scratched at me. I wasn't sure if he was trying to comfort or distract me, but I ignored him.

I didn't sleep that night, and when the sun rose, I gave in and got up, too. A quick shower. A bite of stale toast. A rough comb through my hair. I was out the door earlier than I'd been in a long time. But I had to move quickly if I wanted to bypass Rhys and do some investigating myself. He wasn't going to be happy when he found out, but I wasn't ready to face him yet. My promise to Aelwyn rang in my ears. She'd insisted he could help me, protect me even. Maybe he could, but I wasn't ready.

Havenwood Falls in the morning was gorgeous. A three-hundred-sixty-degree view of mountain peaks with morning fog rolling off them and coating the air in tiny droplets. It was magical in a way that had nothing to do with the fact that this was a town full of supernaturals. In fact, with the sun reflecting off the mist, and the chilled air so clear you could taste it on your tongue, Havenwood Falls felt almost like any other normal ski town. And I felt like any other normal human. As long as said human had found her mother murdered and was the prime suspect in their joke of an investigation.

And just like that, reality crashed back down around me. I turned away from the view I'd been admiring from my second story balcony and made my way down the steps to the street. At the bottom, I jumped back to avoid a collision with a large cardboard cutout of a cartoon cupid drawing its arrow back. It was being carried by two men in handyman uniforms. The one in the back smiled at me and dipped his chin.

"Morning," he said brightly.

I eyed the pink and red hearts painted into the background behind the cardboard cupid and my brows knitted at the familiar coloring and design. "Isn't Valentine's Day still over a week away?" I asked, doing the math in my head.

But he was already gone.

A flash of red hair caught my eye, and I saw Rose Howe smiling wide as she headed for the square with another armful of pink décor. Rose managed Howe's Herbal Shoppe along with the help of her teenaged daughter, Scarlet. Ruby Howe still owned it, but the most she did for that place now was sweep the sidewalk out front while mumbling about talismans and enchantments. I didn't wander too close, mostly because I was afraid Ruby's sixth sense might detect my own ability to enchant.

Rose was harmless enough, aside from her excessive enjoyment for decorating. If a holiday was in sight, you could bet Rose was out here decorating for it. She'd cornered me in my shop two years back and tried to auction me off for a charity date event they'd included in the festivities that year. I'd narrowly avoided it by claiming I had a date of my own somewhere else that night. But then she'd just pried her way in, demanding to know who I was going out with.

I'd given the first name that had come to mind: Ethan. It had shut her up since she didn't know an Ethan, but she was still suspicious of me to this day for it. I couldn't blame her, since I didn't know any Ethan either. At least, not an Ethan that wasn't my magical hawk. But she left me alone after that. Still, I always made sure to steer clear of her this time of year in case she tried roping me in again. An event built around selling people to the highest bidder wasn't my idea of a good time.

"Hi, Gwen," Rose called out as she approached me. "How are you?" Her expression fell in worried concern.

"I'm okay," I said.

Her eyes brimmed with tears, and her chin wobbled. "I heard about Aelwyn, and I'm so very sorry about what happened. We will all miss her very much."

I nodded, suddenly distrustful of my voice at the sight of her watery eyes.

Rose grabbed my arm and squeezed affectionately. "If you need anything at all, please let us know," she added.

"Thanks," I said quietly and looked away. Losing Aelwyn was bad enough, but watching everyone else grieve for her too was too much for me right now.

I cleared my throat and nodded at the decorations Rose carried, forcing my voice lighter. "A little early for decorations, don't you think?" I asked.

"Never too early for romance, Gwen," Rose joked.

I grimaced.

Maybe not, but it was definitely too late.

Aelwyn's final words rang in my ears. She'd told me not to come back to the house, but here I was anyway, completely disregarding her warning. I didn't like going against her, but I was desperate for answers, and if there were any to be found here, I was going to find them. The house was dark, just like I'd left it two nights ago. Even from where I sat in my truck with the cheerful sunshine filtering through the bare branches overhead, it felt lonely. I told myself that was only because I knew she was gone, and then I climbed out of the truck.

The front door had been locked back up since the other night. Rhys, I assumed. I checked the planter by the porch and found the spare key still underneath it. Tucking it into my pocket, I let myself in with my own set. The hinges creaked, but it was a comfort, the familiarity of it.

My phone rang. I glanced down. It was Rhys. No way was I answering him now. If I somehow gave away my location, he'd probably just show up. Instead, I silenced it and ignored the text that followed.

Standing inside the foyer, I inhaled deeply, letting the familiar scent of the house wash over me. There was a bleach smell mixing with it, but I ignored that and concentrated on the scents from my childhood. Grapefruit, for cleaning, my mother would say. Mistletoe for health. And cedar wood. For home. It had always struck me as superstitious and strange—just like her rule about no fae on her property. She'd walk around on weekends sprinkling dried herbs in the corners and onto windowsills, muttering words like she was a witch. I'd rolled my eyes every time.

Now, the memory of it made my chest ache.

My eyes pricked with tears, but I blinked them back and strode through the house and up the stairs to the office. Very deliberately, I ignored the closed bedroom doors—hers and mine—and focused on what I'd come to do. If there was evidence of who could have done this, I would find it. I couldn't afford to give in to grief. Not yet.

For the next two hours, I lost myself in the work of going through all the papers and files Aelwyn had stuffed away up here. Baby pictures, old report cards, and recipes made up most of the desk drawers. Rhys had his own album, and I shoved that aside, determined not to distract myself by reminiscing about happier days. The photos weren't the real story. They didn't tell how he'd broken my heart and my spirit when he'd rejected me. It had never been the same between us after that, and it made me wonder if any of his caring had been real. Maybe I'd just imagined it. Maybe the pictures would prove that if I looked too closely.

I shoved the pictures away, absolutely sure I didn't want to know. Not today.

I poked through the rest of her desk quickly after that. The shelves behind the desk were another matter. Packed full of books, some of them with notes and photos stuffed between pages, the shelves boasted a thin layer of dust and took a lot longer to search through.

When the light coming in the window shifted as the sun climbed toward its high point, I considered breaking for lunch. But no part of me wanted to step foot in that kitchen yet. I went back to work, my stomach grumbling.

I'd nearly given in and decided to come back another day when a book caught my eye. Worn at the edges of the hardcover and blank on the spine, it wasn't familiar to me. I pulled at it gingerly until it slipped from the shelf and fell into my hands. But when I turned the cover, I blinked in surprise. The inside was hollow. It wasn't a book at all.

A hiding place, I realized.

Folded and ancient-looking, a small slip of paper lay inside.

I took it out and unfolded it, leaning on the book case as I opened it and read the scrawled words. The further I read, the colder I became. It was from a woman named Moonlaith. The language she used was formal, but the tone was so personal and emotional, I knew they must have been close.

MAKE sure she eats the mistletoe at least once a week. And the cedar wood. To protect the magic that lives inside her skin. I know you will protect our daughter with your life, Ael. We are eternally grateful for your sacrifice, dear friend. Should you need us, the Protector can send word. And if we do not meet again in this life, we will reunite in the next. She is special, Ael. Too gentle for them and too strong for the life we would give her here. When the time comes, she will not have to hide. They will hide from her. When the time is right, tell her what she is so she will understand all we have done.

With love,
Moonlaith

I READ it over and over again, stunned. My entire life, I'd believed my parents had given me up, left me on Aelwyn's doorstep as an infant and never looked back. They were unknowns. Even when I'd grown old enough to try to dig up any information on my own, the town records left no trace of them. But this woman spoke as if she knew Aelwyn well. As if Aelwyn knew her.

And who was I supposed to be hiding from? Aelwyn had said they'd never stopped hunting me. My stomach tightened at the idea that someone might have killed Aelwyn to get to me.

The letter shook in my hands.

It took a long moment before I realized it wasn't the letter shaking. It was me.

I looked up, staring out the window, unseeing as the questions threatened to drown me. The woman had mentioned a protector. Whoever it was, they had access to my mother. I needed to find that person. To find the truth.

My arm itched as Ethan stirred, his claws scratching at my skin until I turned irritably toward him. "What?" I hissed.

There was no answer, but movement outside the window caught my eye, and I jerked my head to the glass just as a figure turned away. A blur of red cloth flashed boldly through the bare branches below. With a sharp breath, I shoved the letter into my cargo pocket and bolted down the stairs and out the door.

The moment we hit the open air, Ethan peeled away from my arm and swooped up and overhead. His sharp cry pierced the air, and I shushed him with my mind, listening for anything else that moved or spoke. Just like two nights ago, the house disappeared behind me and the woods closed in. This time, I had daylight to guide me.

I slowed and took better care to move quietly. Fae were good at stealth, but I'd been too panicked and too intent on catching up to whoever it was to take care. Now, I could only hope it hadn't been a trap, because I'd played right into it, announcing my presence like a steamroller. Or a human.

But that face . . . For a split second, it had almost looked like—

But it couldn't be. Aelwyn was gone.

A few minutes later, the woods were silent around me, and the only scent I caught came from the neighbor to the west. A human couple. Elderly. No children or pets. Even Ethan had come up empty. Whatever had been here earlier, it was gone now. And now I had to admit I'd lost the lead for a second time. I doubled back to the house, swearing to myself and to Aelwyn there wouldn't be a third.

CHAPTER 5

*T*wo days passed quietly. I worked and ate and slept—all the while waiting for Rhys or Ada or even the police to come sniffing around. But none of them did. I felt like I was being watched, but every time I turned to look or tried peeking out my windows, there was nothing there. Ethan remained uneasy, so I knew it wasn't all in my head, but I also had no idea what to do about it. Grief set in, causing me to tear up every time something small and stupid reminded me of my mother. I kept the tears at bay with a small tattoo I inked onto on my right hip. A box of tissues that, when directed properly, did the trick to keep my emotions at bay while I worked.

It was the first magical tattoo I'd given myself in years. Ada's claims about the mountain lion had spooked me, but after no visits from the police or any more news, I forced the issue from my mind. Besides, Aelwyn would have loved that I'd used my gift, and that made it okay somehow.

By the third day, I was starting to grow impatient with the police. They said they'd reach out when the investigation would allow me to pick up Aelwyn's body, and I needed to make arrangements for her burial.

I woke to my alarm and dressed quickly, intent on a cup of coffee before making my way to the police station that sat around the corner next to City Hall.

As I walked, the back of my neck prickled with a strange sort of awareness. Someone was watching me. No, scratch that. Everyone was watching me. Or maybe not watching but seeing. Three different people stopped to say hello and ask how I was doing as I passed them on my walk to Broastful Brew. That never happened.

In fact, ever since my Awakening a few years ago, when I'd come into my fae powers, most residents of Havenwood Falls had made it a point to avoid me completely. It was as if I wasn't even there. Unless they came looking for a tattoo. But that was another matter.

Today, something was different. The way Mabel, the coffee shop's owner, smiled at me as she said "good morning" was wrong somehow. It felt like too big a gesture. Or maybe I was just grumpy pre-coffee.

"Hot damn, where did you get those boots? They're awesome."

I turned slowly at the voice. "Are you talking to me?" I asked, shocked to find the girl behind me blinking expectantly.

She smiled. "Yeah, those boots are rad. I love the vintage vibe. Did you get them at Callie's?"

"Uh. No. Amazon."

She laughed. "That was my second guess." Before I could respond, she leaned in and whispered, "We'll let this be our secret, though. Wouldn't want to make Callie think she was losing her edge."

I nodded in agreement. Callie's Consignments was the local spot for anything vintage. She did get some cool pieces from time to time, but buying something would have required I interact with actual people. Something I tried to avoid at all costs. And usually it wasn't difficult —until now.

Did I know this girl? Maybe we'd met and I'd forgotten?

"I recognize you from your shop, Tragic Ink. You know, if you're looking for some help—"

"Listen, I hate to cut this short, but I have some place to be."

"Sure, yeah, no problem." She waved me off with a bright smile. "Nice to meet you."

"You, too," I managed before slipping out the door and into the sunshine, coffee in hand. A twinge of guilt twisted in my gut at how rude I'd been to the girl. She seemed nice, actually, in that overly friendly way that could sometimes be annoying. It would have been great with the customers. But I'd had an intern once, last summer, and while Cole was talented, it hadn't gone well, despite the convenience of having someone else do my coffee runs. I wasn't ready to take on another.

I let the cardboard cup warm my fingers as I walked, using my free hand to pull my hat low over my forehead. Head down, I blazed a trail across the street and inside the police station, determined to get there without another "friendly" encounter.

What was wrong with people today?

THE RECEPTIONIST at the front desk took my name and information and disappeared through a door behind her glass window. When she didn't return right away, I wandered into the waiting area and took a seat.

Several minutes passed.

And then several more.

I tapped my fingers against my thigh and drank my coffee. When it was gone, I got up, tossed the cup, and began pacing. Finally, I sat again.

By the time the door opened, my mood had turned dark and my patience was wearing thin.

Deputy Conall stood in the open doorway that separated the seating area from the receptionist's desk. His eyes were distant and his smile forced. Overly polite. "Miss Facharro. What can I do for you?"

I stood up. "I'd like a status update on my foster mother's case. I was supposed to hear back when it was clear for me to have her picked up. I need to make arrangements with the funeral home and a transport to take her to—"

"I'm sorry, Miss Facharro," he cut me off, frowning now. The smile—and the politeness—were gone. "Your foster mother's remains have already been released."

I grimaced at his casual reference to her "remains," but then his words sank in, and I blinked. "Released? When? To who?"

He consulted the scrap of paper again, but it didn't seem to hold the answers he was looking for. "I, uh, I'm not sure exactly. I was off yesterday, so I would have to put in a request to check."

"A request to . . . Are you kidding me? I'm her family. There's no one else you could have possibly released her to!" Well, me and Rhys, but he would have told me. Right? I thought of the unanswered calls and texts from him, but then shoved that thought away. The only thing that mattered was Aelwyn's last rites and wishes—and the fact that I should have been involved in facilitating both.

"All due respect, ma'am, you're not really her relative. The law dictates a relative is bloodline—"

"I don't give a shit what the law dictates." On my arm, Ethan clawed and whined at the heat that crept over me as my temper spiked and flared. I ignored both my familiar and my own conscience that whispered against losing my shit on an officer of the law. In the police station. Especially when it was very likely I was still a suspect. But I couldn't stop myself. The woman who had been a mother to me was gone. They'd given her body to someone who wasn't me. And now I would never see her again.

"Be that as it may—" Deputy Conall began.

"She was my legal guardian, and as such, I have every right to her. Including the information about her killer—who, by the way, is not me." My voice rose, and it was all I could do not to unleash enough magic along with my words to send a real message. Several of the tattoos etched along my skin burned and tingled, practically begging to be used. I noted it absently, and in the back of my mind, surprise registered. Those tattoos had never stirred before. "Now, you run back to Sheriff Kasun and tell him I want a phone call by end of day with whatever information he has on her case and the name of the person her body was released to. Otherwise, I'll take up the legalities with the Court. You got that?"

"I . . . Yes, ma'am. I've got it." His expression was tight-lipped, but he didn't argue.

I spun on my heel and stormed out.

CHAPTER 6

$\mathcal{B}$y the time I walked off the worst of my temper, the sun was high in the sky and traffic in the square was bustling. In preparation for Valentine's Day, the gazebo had already been decorated with fresh red roses and climbing vines that had been woven through the railing. The lattice I'd seen being delivered yesterday had been set up and more climbing roses decorated that, creating a selfie station for pedestrians to stop at. Despite the chill in the air, the color and energy was cheerful. Too cheerful. It only made my dark mood feel even more tempestuous.

To top it off, people were still nodding and smiling softly at me as I passed by. Some of them even whispered a hello or an "I'm sorry for your loss." Miss Mary Beth stopped me and asked what time I'd be home later, so she could drop off a casserole. She was too nice to argue with, so I made the arrangements, secretly a little comforted that so many people wanted to show how much they'd cared about Aelwyn. But it also served as a nonstop reminder that she was gone.

My own grief was heavier by the time Miss Mary Beth had disappeared and I'd turned toward my shop. These people were grieving for Aelwyn, same as I was, but watching them do it only made my own pain worse. To keep from crying, I let it piss me off. God, what the hell was wrong with people today? When did everyone become so damn friendly?

My phone rang, and I answered with a clipped, "Hello?"

"Miss Facharro, Sheriff Kasun here. You asked for a phone call." He didn't sound happy to be fulfilling my request, and that could only mean he knew why I'd asked him to call—and how I felt about it.

"Yes. I'd like to know who you released Aelwyn to and why you think you could just—"

"She was released to Rhys Graywalk, her oldest living relative per the legal code on guardianship."

I blinked. "What?"

"Rhys Graywalk. Aelwyn was his legal guardian, right?" He spoke slower now, like he was waiting for his words to sink in.

"Yes."

He sighed. "And he's older than you, correct?"

I didn't answer. We both knew that he was.

"Miss Facharro, I am sorry you were in the dark on this, but that's something you'll have to take up with Rhys." When I still didn't answer, he cleared his throat. "I am sorry for your loss."

"Thanks," I said in a wavering voice and then hung up.

A quick scroll through my texts confirmed what I'd already suspected. Rhys had tried to reach out, several times actually. Two of the texts he'd sent had specifically asked me to call about making Aelwyn's arrangements, and I'd ignored them all. This was my own fault.

I reached the alley and shoved my way through the throng of people that loitered on the stairs leading up to my shop.

It wasn't until I reached the front door to Tragic Ink that I realized the loiterers on the stairs weren't just hanging out for fun. This was a line. And they were all waiting to enter my shop.

"Oh, there she is," said one of the men near the front. "That's Gwen. The owner." Ricky, a bear shifter I remembered from high school, pointed me out to the crowd from where he stood second in line. "You have any appointments available today?" he asked eagerly.

"Um. I . . . need to . . ." I didn't finish answering him before I shoved him and the man in front of him out of the way and unlocked the door. Then I slipped inside and closed the door behind me before they could follow. A few called out protests and whined at being kept waiting.

I locked the deadbolt and didn't bother with the lights as I strode to the back cabinet where I kept a stash of whiskey. The first shot went down harsh, burning a trail down my throat and into my empty stomach. The second was smoother and calmed the worst of the storm inside me.

I did my best to shove aside thoughts of Aelwyn—and what I wanted to do to the person who had murdered her. For the first time in years, the temptation to ink myself with a magical tat made for harm was strong. A vat of acid, a plate of rat poison—a bullet would have been too good for whoever it was. But then I pulled myself up short. Killing was not the answer. And I was not a murderer.

Someone else was, though.

I had no idea who in Havenwood Falls was capable of that, and it was nearly impossible for an outsider to gain that kind of access to the town without tripping an alarm—all of the boundaries were spelled for that kind of thing and the Court's magic was strong. Surely, they would know if someone had breached their wards and snuck inside the borders. Regardless, I would be the last to know if something like that happened.

I sighed.

Rhys was right. I couldn't do this alone. I needed help. And someone who had access to information. I had no idea if he did, but he was the only one who believed in my innocence. In fact, without Aelwyn, Rhys was the only person I had left in the world, and that, I realized, was depressing as hell.

Ten minutes later, the whiskey had served its purpose. I was calm enough to realize I needed help and just depressed enough about that fact to realize the line outside my shop was a perfect distraction until I could talk to Rhys. I knew for a fact his working hours nearly matched mine exactly thanks to the bar he owned and ran near the ski area. Resigned and more than a little cautious, I pulled my appointment book out and unlocked the front door.

The next four hours passed quickly. The first hour was nothing but scheduling as I worked my way through the line of people outside. It was a first, having my calendar full like this. I told myself it was a good thing, that having the bills paid on time would be a nice change, but this sudden influx of attention still had me suspicious. Four people had the balls to ask me how much I charged for the magical ink. The first three left easily enough when I told them to get the hell out without confirming or denying my ability. The fourth wasn't so easy.

The man stood with hands out, pleading at me from the other side of the front counter. "Look, I'll pay whatever you ask. I just need—"

"I said I don't do that." I leaned over the counter, planting my hands for more leverage as I got in his face. "And if you don't leave now, the only magic I'll infuse into your tattoo is the blood I'll draw when I stab you with my favorite pen."

He left quickly after that, still muttering. I crossed my fingers he wasn't the type to report bodily threats. That wouldn't go over well with the police right now.

The next few hours were spent inking new customers. The first wanted a ladder with initials carved into each of the rungs. I had no idea why, and I didn't question it. Probably a family or lineage thing; I'd seen my share of those. It was a cool idea, but after the morning I'd had, conversation was the last thing I wanted.

When the next customer wouldn't stop attempting small talk, I told him I worked best in silence. He finally shut up, and the rest of the evening passed quickly.

At ten, I closed the door behind the last client and flipped the sign, turning the deadbolt just in case. By the time I'd cleaned up, the couple of shots I'd taken had long since worn off, and my stomach growled and twisted in defiance at being left empty. A diet of coffee and booze didn't sit well. Or maybe it was the knowledge that I was about to willingly visit the Dirty Knuckle.

I needed food.

And time to figure out how to approach Rhys.

THE DIRTY KNUCKLE was a brick building with soft lighting and lots of dark leather. I'd been inside once. A personal test two years ago to see if I was really over Rhys like I'd been telling myself for so long. Thirty minutes in a corner booth that obscured me from the bar and the back offices had proved otherwise. I hadn't been back since, though I was ashamed to admit that I knew for a fact he was there now. Just like I knew he was there every day during the same hours I was at Tragic. I knew more about Rhys Graywalk than I'd ever let on. But, this time at least, it worked to my advantage.

I sat in the same booth as last time, needing the view of the bar and offices it provided. The dark leather was cold against my jeans, so I took my jacket off and slid it underneath me to warm my legs.

Across the room, I spotted Michaela Petran sitting with her fiancé,

Xandru, and her best friend, Addie Beaumont. The three of them had been practically inseparable since Michaela had returned to Havenwood Falls almost a year ago. I'd gone to high school with them, and Addie and I were still friends.

Addie was the official tattoo artist for the Court, a job I wouldn't want in a million years because it meant taking orders, but Addie seemed to enjoy it. She was also an amazing artist, and her friendliness could somehow cut through my layers of grumpy self-defense. She was actually a fun drinking buddy when I felt like getting out, but I wasn't in the mood to socialize tonight. When Addie glanced my way, I made sure to keep my eyes averted and my ski cap pulled low. She must have taken the hint because, thankfully, none of them came over to say hello.

A moment later, a server with a nametag that read Casten took my order. He was fae, older than me by maybe ten years. I didn't know more than that, but like recognized like; it was easy to spot my own kind around here.

And he was friendly—just like the rest of the damned town today.

I grunted answers, making it clear I didn't want to chat, then wolfed down a burger and fries. While I ate, I watched for Rhys and eventually lost myself in the hum of voices and laughter as the human tourist crowd piled in from the ski resort just down the road. It felt good to be anonymous again. Maybe I'd come here more often if the locals didn't let up on their new friendly routine. Unless Rhys chased me away again.

Casten had just cleared my plate and brought me a beer when I spotted him. Rhys emerged from the offices behind the bar area, smiling and chatting with a couple of men seated on leather stools. I recognized one of them as Everett Weston, a gargoyle who'd moved to town about a year ago. Rhys was great at making new friends and maintaining them, not like me with my former classmates. I'd always liked that about him, like we balanced each other out somehow. Yin and yang.

But now . . . I'd never felt less close to him.

From here, I could see his dark hair falling over his forehead nearly to his eyes. I had no idea when he'd started growing it out, but I liked it better that way. It made him look younger but still dangerous. Sexy. The thought brought me up short. This visit was not about the way Rhys wore his hair. It couldn't be. It was about mutual cooperation. It was about finding a killer.

It was about justice, and that was it.

As if I'd called his name aloud, Rhys suddenly looked up, the easy smile he'd worn a moment ago frozen on his face as he spotted me. Our eyes met and held. The smile vanished. In its place was a storm that reminded me of my own dark mood from this morning.

Good. My temper was going to come in handy now that it had a target. I latched on to my anger, still simmering underneath the surface, and slid to my feet. When Rhys cocked his head at me, I grabbed my jacket and made my way over, leaving my empty beer glass behind.

"Hey," he said. Relief, surprise, and a lot of what might have been hope was packed into the single word.

"Hi." My response was short. Hopefully impossible to read.

He gestured toward the office door behind him, and I slipped inside, my expression arranged into something hard as I scanned the space before me. I'd never been in here before, nor had I seen Rhys in his personal space in several years now, but it was somehow exactly what I pictured for him. The office was done in dark leather and warm earth tones. Deep-cushioned chairs that complemented a dark-stained desk took up the center of the room. Along the wall was a leather sofa worn into soft creases. Landscape prints of the forest hung above it. Across from the sofa, a fire blazed in the hearth. The effect was masculine and still somehow cozy.

I wanted to hate it out of spite, and because I didn't, that fueled my temper too.

When the door clicked shut behind me, I whirled and found Rhys watching me, his dark eyes warming when they settled on mine.

"Gwen," he said simply, but the single word sent a thousand emotions rippling through me. It was so warm and personal, like an invitation. Like he was telling me a secret. "It's good to see you here."

I could tell he meant it, and that hurt. My temper flared, thanks to the pang of hurt. "I wish I could say the same."

He didn't react to the harshness of my words except to nod as if he'd expected nothing less. I bristled at the easy way he gestured to the sofa. "Would you like to sit?"

"What I would like are answers," I said.

"We have that in common, then."

I blinked. Whatever I'd expected him to say, that wasn't it. "All right," I said uncertainly.

"You've thought over my offer?"

"I have." My shoulders sagged, and I couldn't shake the feeling that I was admitting a loss. "And we should do it. Work together, I mean."

I blinked, realizing he'd wandered closer. When I took a step back, he frowned. The heat of the fire warmed the back of my legs.

"What?" I demanded when he didn't say anything.

He cocked his head, peering at me. "Are you still taking the mistletoe —your vitamins, I mean?"

"My— What the hell does that have to do with anything?"

"You look a little tired. I just want to be sure you're taking care of yourself."

I didn't miss the fact that he'd mentioned mistletoe—the same thing that mysterious letter had mentioned—or the way he'd just changed the subject, like he'd said too much.

"Of course I'm tired," I snap back at him. "I've just lost the only mother I've ever known. And what the hell do you know about mistletoe?"

He took a step closer again, this time invading my space, and my pulse thrummed wildly. But Rhys was scanning me head to toe as if on alert, completely oblivious to the fact that his smell had invaded my senses and made it hard to remember what the hell we were even talking about.

"Something happened," he said, his brows dipping in concern.

I lifted my chin, determined not to react to his closeness. "I went to the police today to ask about collecting Aelwyn's remains. They said she's gone. Apparently, they released her to you already, so I'm here now to discuss her arrangements. I think we should bury her in the cemetery behind—"

"Gwen, stop for a second."

"What?"

Rhys looked away, and there was something about his expression that sent alarm bells off in my head.

"Do you have something else in mind?" I asked.

"We can't bury Aelwyn in town," he said quietly.

"What are you talking about? Where else would we bury her?"

"Nowhere. She'll be cremated," he said.

"What?" I stepped back. "You can't just decide something like that without me. Look, I know I didn't return your texts about the arrangements, but you could have told me you'd already picked her up. I had to find out from Deputy Conall, who by the way, has a shitty bedside manner."

Rhys sighed. "I'm sorry. You weren't returning my texts or calls, and I couldn't wait any longer."

"Wait for what?" I demanded. My heart thudded hard in my chest as I stared at his tight expression. There was something he wasn't telling me here, something more. "What have you done with Aelwyn, Rhys?"

"She's been returned to the Seelie Court," he said gently.

"What do you mean 'returned' to the Seelie Court?"

Rhys spoke gently. "It was her wish to return to her homeland when she . . ."

He didn't say the words, but I couldn't appreciate his sensitivity. Not when I was still processing what he'd just said. Like he knew for sure that's where she'd gone because he'd been a part of it. And I didn't just mean now that she was gone. He'd known about this all along, and he'd kept it from me. No wonder Aelwyn had told me to go to Rhys. They'd been in on whatever this was together.

My pulse raced faster now, but it had nothing to do with attraction and everything to do with fear. Rhys was holding back. And if there was some lie, some secret he was keeping, I needed to know. I damn sure couldn't let him betray me twice.

"How do you know all this?" I demanded, my voice low to keep it from shaking.

"Because," he said, "I took her there myself last night. I used the portal that brought her here almost twenty years ago. The same portal that brought you here with her. The same portal that brought me when I was ten." His voice was sad, and I knew he was bracing himself for the truth he was about to admit. "We're all three from Faerie, Gwen. And we're connected in ways you don't yet know. But I think . . . it's time to tell you. Aelwyn would want that, and I can't keep you safe any longer without admitting the truth."

"What truth?" I asked.

"The truth about who you really are."

"And who am I?" I asked.

Rhys took a deep breath. "You're Gwenllian, a member of the Seelie royal court. Your father was a warrior, a Protector. You inherited your gift with the ink from your mother. She uses her gift to fight for the Seelie Court in the war against the Unseelie. The dark fae have been after her for years, hoping to take her power for themselves. Hoping to take you. Your parents sent you here as a baby in order to hide you from Unseelie spies."

"How do you know all of this?" I asked.

"It was part of my mission to know."

"Your mission . . ." I repeated, my voice breaking underneath the weight of my grief. Aelwyn was gone, but Rhys was here, and he was breaking my heart all over again. Everything I thought I knew about myself, about her, about him, was a lie.

CHAPTER 7

"Say something," Rhys said quietly.

But I couldn't. All I could do was blink back the tears and put one foot in front of the other, my gaze locked on the door behind him. But a hand on my wrist stopped me just before I reached the knob. Rhys squeezed and yanked, twisting me back to face him. Instead of anger, I found desperation in his eyes.

"Say something," he repeated, this time pleading.

"There's nothing left to say." My voice sounded strangely ragged, even to me.

"There's everything left to say," he argued stubbornly.

"And you've had my entire life to say it."

He flinched. "Let me explain."

"I don't want to hear it." My shoulders sagged with real defeat this time. Rhys had won again, though the prize was twisted: my broken heart.

"You do," he insisted, tugging on my hand—and I let him because it struck me that I couldn't remember the last time I'd touched his skin. Even after all the lies, that's what I noticed. "Five minutes, Gwen. Give me five minutes, and after that, if you want to walk out of here, I won't stop you."

I eyed him. A beat of silence passed.

"You're not the only one who lost her, you know." His voice broke.

I watched as a single tear leaked from the corner of his eye, and my heart ached at the sight of it. He was right. Lies or not, he'd lost Aelwyn too, and I knew he'd loved her just as much as I had.

"Five minutes," I whispered.

Rhys nodded and blew out a breath. "Okay. The truth is that your parents sent Aelwyn here, with you, from Faerie. The dark fae had tracked you all, and your parents knew you weren't safe with them anymore. They used their fae contacts here on the Court to get approval and help erase any paper trail of your arrival or the names of your real family. Aelwyn gave you her last name as another way to throw the dark fae off your trail. She was vigilant with her wards and careful to keep out any fae she hadn't personally vetted. Everything she did was to keep you safe all these years."

I felt my knees wobble and threaten to buckle as I thought back to how adamant Aelwyn had always been about strange fae coming around. "How do you know so much? Did Aelwyn tell you all of this?"

"She did, but that's not the reason I know." He hesitated, his gaze flicking from my face to my legs. "You should sit."

Without waiting for a response, he walked behind his desk and opened a drawer. He drew out a couple of glasses and a bottle of amber liquid decorated with a label I didn't recognize. Not bothering to ask first, he poured a shot and handed it to me. I took it and sank onto the edge of the couch without a word, watching as he poured one for himself and then knocked it back. When it was gone, he immediately refilled the glass.

After a long moment, Rhys continued, "I was born in Faerie. Both of my parents were soldiers for the Seelie Court there. When I was five, they were both killed in a skirmish with Unseelie mercenaries."

"God, Rhys, I'm sorry. I didn't know." The words were out before I could stop them. The feeling of loss was too raw and too familiar not to feel empathy for him. All this time I'd known him and he'd never told me this. So many other things, but not this.

He nodded slowly, and I could see the grief it still caused him. "Thank you. After that, I was drafted into the junior academy. A training program for future fae soldiers. I worked hard, determined to avenge my parents, and because of that, my performance stood out. When I was ten, I was chosen for a smaller team, and I graduated from that as a Protector."

Protector. Just like the letter from my mother had described. I took a deep breath, my heart pounding. "What's a Protector?"

"We're what you might call a bodyguard. We're tasked with keeping a specific fae safe. Our missions are usually more dangerous than a soldier's, because we're on our own without backup. We're the only one standing between our assignment and the threat."

"Kind of like Secret Service then?"

He nodded and hesitated before adding, "I was tasked with protecting you."

"Me?" Shock, confusion, and anger were a chaotic cloud inside me. Quickly, I did the math, counting back to how old he'd been when he'd come to Aelwyn. He'd only been ten years old when they'd given him the assignment? I vaguely remembered him moving in with us around that time, and we'd become fast friends. In fact, by the time I'd grown into my power, he'd been my only friend.

All this time, and he'd never let on . . .

Rhys set his glass aside and knelt in front of me. "Your gift, Gwen, with the ink. The tattoos . . . You're very special. There are enemies of the Seelie Court that want that gift so they can use it for their own gain."

"Those enemies, the dark fae you were talking about," I said grimly. "That's who Aelwyn was hiding me from."

"Yes."

"The night she died, she mentioned it. But I was only a baby when I left. How would they know I have this gift?"

Rhys grimaced. "We suspect they didn't know for sure. But since your mother has it and your father was a seer, they're betting you're going to be valuable to them in some way."

"And now that they found Aelwyn, they know for sure," I finished.

Rhys didn't answer.

"My gift," I repeated, twisting the word with as much cynicism as I could muster. "More like a curse." Rhys opened his mouth to respond, but I redirected—mostly because I was not ready to address any of the crazy, unbelievable things he'd just said about who I was and where I really came from. "Tell me where you took Aelwyn. Tell me how to get there."

"There's a portal about three miles northwest of Aelwyn's house. It leads directly to the outskirts of the Seelie Court's territory, where Aelwyn is from. Last night, I took her through it and delivered her to the Seelie guard on the other side."

"You actually went to Faerie . . ." I wanted to ask about my real mother, but I held back. I couldn't let my emotions run away with me.

Not now. Not while I still needed answers. "How? Wouldn't the Court here sense the portal opening?"

He nodded. "They did. I had authorization, so it wasn't a problem."

I stared at him, but it was like staring at a stranger now. He'd gotten special permission from the Court to open a portal? The only way he could have managed that was if everything he had said were true. He was a Protector. A special agent from beyond the veil sent here for the sole purpose of protecting me from the worst of the worst. Like Ada. I snorted. No, whoever was after me was worse than Ada. That made me shudder.

"What happened to make them send you here?" I asked.

"What do you mean?"

"For ten years, it was just Aelwyn and me. So, did something happen for them to think we needed you? Did someone come after me?"

"No. You had another Protector. An older fae named Leif. He lived just past Fred and Betsy, the human couple next door."

"Oh." I let that sink in, remembering the older man Aelwyn had mentioned when I was younger. A friend of hers who liked to bring us fresh vegetables from the farmer's market in town, until one day he just stopped coming around. I barely remembered him now.

"When you were six, Leif retired, and I was sent in his place."

"You were only ten," I said, still a little stunned that he'd received a mission so young.

"My age was an advantage they believed outweighed my inexperience."

I snarled, the betrayal twisting further. "Because they knew you and I would be friends."

His expression mirrored the pain I felt. "Gwen—"

"Was any of it real?"

"What?" he asked.

"Our friendship. Was it all part of your mission to make me trust you? To make me spend time with you. Or was any of it real?"

"Gwen." He softened. "Of course it was real. Every second of it was absolutely real. You are everything to me."

His words sounded so sincere, but I couldn't reconcile them with his rejection. I gripped the glass tightly in my hand, desperate not to relive the moment that had ended our friendship three years earlier. "What was my mother's name?"

"What?" Rhys blinked at me.

I scowled. "If you want me to believe what you're saying is true, then you need to give me something I can verify. What was my real mother's name?"

"I don't see how that will help you verify anything. It's not on any records here."

"Humor me."

Rhys sighed. "Her name is Moonlaith."

The words were so soft. So certain. And an exact match to the name on the strange letter I'd uncovered in Aelwyn's study. Which meant Rhys wasn't lying. Not about any of it. Knowing that didn't make this any easier.

"Wow. The letter was real," I whispered.

Rhys rose from where he'd crouched and slid onto the sofa next to me. "What letter?"

"I found a letter when I was going through Aelwyn's things . . ." In a halting voice, I told him what it had said. And the name that was scrawled at the bottom.

"It's true. Moonlaith is your mother," he confirmed.

"Is?" I tensed. "You mean she's still alive?"

"Yes."

"And my father? You said he was a seer?"

Rhys looked away.

"Rhys?"

When he turned back to me, his expression was pained. "Gwen, he . . ."

I swallowed hard. "Just tell me the truth, Rhys."

"He was a seer," Rhys agreed quietly. "He was also your mother's Protector. According to the report, he saw the dark fae coming for you. You weren't going to make it out, so he stayed behind to buy you some time. He was killed defending you and Aelwyn on the day you were both smuggled into Havenwood Falls. I'm sorry."

"It's okay. I . . . Thank you for telling me," I said. He nodded, and I bit my lip. "But my mother . . . you could contact her? Could we maybe go through the portal and see her?"

"Yes, I—" He frowned at the sight of my face. "Gwen, hold on. It's not safe right now, okay? When this is all over, I promise you, I'll take you to see her, but not until then."

"Okay." I forced myself to relax and focus on the rest of what my mother had written. "So it's true about the mistletoe?"

Rhys nodded. "The mistletoe keeps others from detecting your gift. Actually, according to Aelwyn, it also keeps people from really noticing you or becoming too interested. Another protection."

I gaped at him. "Is that why everyone's being so damn friendly lately? Because I stopped taking the mistletoe?"

He shrugged, but the half smirk he gave confirmed my suspicions. "You have something against folks being neighborly?"

I leaned back, stunned. "All this time, I thought she was just a health nut. Always shoving herbal supplements at me and insisting they were vitamins."

"Well, they are good for you."

I glared. "You knew all this time, and you never told me. And neither did she." More than anything, I wished Aelwyn was still here to defend herself. To hug me. To let me forgive her. How did you forgive a dead person?

"After your Awakening, Aelwyn wanted to tell you, but I had orders. I took an oath, Gwen. I couldn't break that without permission. It was too dangerous. And Aelwyn respected that, even if she didn't like it. That's why she didn't tell you about her burial wishes. I'm sorry I went behind your back about that, but I couldn't do anything that would break my oath."

"And now? Why are you telling me now?"

"Because your safety trumps everything. Even the oath. Even . . . my feelings."

I hadn't expected him to go there—and because he'd surprised me, I faltered. For a split second, I knew my emotions showed on my face. By the time I'd rearranged my features, Rhys had leaned in, his warm hand resting on my knee. His dark eyes were intense and stormy and full of . . . whatever it was that had made me ever think he cared about me like I'd cared about him.

"I don't want to talk about it," I mumbled.

"Gwen, I know I hurt you. I'm so sorry for that. But . . . I couldn't let it go that far. My oath forbade—"

I shook my head. "You don't have to explain."

"I do. I should have explained a long time ago. The kiss . . ."

"Was a mistake," I finished for both of us, and in one swig, I knocked back the liquid in my glass, welcoming the burn that followed. It was sharp enough to drown out the twinge of pain in my chest my own words had caused.

"No." Rhys grabbed my leg and pulled me closer, shifting me so that we were knee to knee—and eye to eye. His swirled with emotion. Mine . . . I wasn't sure what I looked like now, except that I was terrified and breathless and completely mesmerized by him. Again. I swallowed hard against the pounding in my chest. He could hear it, I was sure of that. "Gwen, that kiss was so much better than any of the times I'd imagined it happening."

"You . . . imagined it?"

"Of course." His expression softened. His lips curved into a smile, and I couldn't tear my gaze away from his mouth. "I've wanted you probably since the moment I saw you. Even at ten, when girls weren't on my radar, you always managed to get my attention. You were my favorite person before the end of that first week at Aelwyn's house. By high school, I was a lost cause. You were way too skinny, with legs too long for the rest of you. But you had this passion and fire that lit you from the inside out. You were all I thought about. Still are."

His hand came up to cup my face, and I tried not to lean into his calloused fingertips as they stroked my cheek. I shuddered as he leaned in.

"What about the oath?" I whispered.

"Screw the oath." His lips were only a breath away now. "I shouldn't have let it ruin this. I want you back in my life. It's been hell without you."

I wasn't even sure I was breathing anymore.

A sharp cramp in my hip sent me jerking, my spine curving until my entire body was pulled taut. I gasped as one of my tattoos came to life, stretching and growling as it animated against my skin.

"Damn it," I said between clenched teeth.

Rhys's brows dipped, and he leaned away as I spasmed again. "What's wrong?"

"The fucking hellhound." I shoved to my feet, peeling my shirt back to reveal the canine I suspected would be shifting and shimmering as it moved against the canvas of my right ribcage. I didn't need to remove my clothes for the ink to break free, but I needed to be sure which tattoo had begun to wake up.

Rhys stared, eyes wide, and his breath whooshed out as he watched the tattoo come to life on my skin. "Holy shit, Gwen. I mean, I knew you could . . . that they were . . . I've just never actually seen your ink come to life," he finally finished.

I gritted my teeth against the pain as the hound scratched and tore, trying to break free from where it had been stretched from my side to my back—an exact replica of the one I'd inked on a client almost four years ago now. It was one of the scarier magical tats I'd done before I'd realized how deadly the consequences could be if activated in the wrong hands. There were only a few still floating around unused out there that could actually do serious harm. The rest were either for Ada—and I didn't like to think about those—or harmless. I'd hoped after this long, maybe the hellhound would never actually be used.

I was wrong.

"What is it?" Rhys asked, his grin vanishing as he took in the horror-struck expression I gave him.

"I gave that tattoo to Walter Glass a couple of years ago."

"Looks like someone pissed him off pretty bad tonight." Rhys looked back at me, his expression grave. "Will it be like last time?"

My body hummed in dread at the thought. "Maybe. We have to go," I said, grabbing my jacket and heading for the door.

Rhys jumped up, and rather than stop me, he followed on my heels. "I'm driving."

I steeled myself against the pain, hoping like hell I'd make it outside before this thing peeled away from me.

"Fine," I said, breathless with the effort of holding the ink inside my skin. I was too distracted to care when Rhys pressed his hand to the small of my back, leading me though the busy bar and into the night.

When he steered me to his truck rather than my own, I let him. Mentally, I listed out all the reasons why this time wasn't the same as last time. There weren't nearly enough to convince me, though. We were together, we'd been about to kiss, and I was still just as much in love with Rhys Graywalk as I'd ever been. I could only pray history wasn't about to repeat itself; that whoever was on the receiving end of this hellhound would live through it.

Inside the truck, Rhys cranked the engine and peeled out, asking, "Where to?"

"I don't know yet. The tattoo is going to . . . peel off my skin," I said through gritted teeth. "When it does, it will try to find its way to the other half."

"Will it obey you like the bird does?"

"No. This one's different. It doesn't belong to me, so I don't control it. I just get a carbon copy."

"What will it do once it's free?"

"It will try to join itself. We need to follow it wherever it goes and try to stop it from hurting someone."

"Will it be solid?" he asked.

I understood his question and shook my head. "No. It will be life size, but only the original is solid. That's the one we have to stop." *Kill.* I meant kill, but I couldn't say the word. Not so soon after Aelwyn.

"Okay," Rhys said, his gaze hard. His eyes glinted in the darkness of the truck, and I didn't miss the edge of danger he wore now like a second skin. I'd never seen him fight, but I knew instinctively in that moment that Rhys could take down anyone or anything that threatened me.

Anything but my own magic, anyway. No one could save me from that.

The thought depressed me. But then the pain took over again, and everything else faded. The hellhound was seconds away from separating itself from my body. Which meant the magic being used to activate it was almost complete. This time, I let it happen. When the ink on my side disappeared, I blinked and looked up. Through the window of the truck, I saw it pass through the passenger door beside me and out onto the empty street beyond. Nothing more than a gray shadow of a creature, but I knew better than anyone how lethal it would be against whatever it was aimed at.

"There," I said. "He's headed for the west side of town."

"Shit," Rhys breathed again as he stared at the ghostly form of the hellhound. "He's fast."

"We have to hurry, Rhys," I urged.

Rhys blinked, then punched the gas, and we shot off.

If we were lucky, we'd get there in time to stop history from repeating itself. If we weren't . . . someone else might die tonight. And it was all my fault. My gift had once again become a curse.

CHAPTER 8

My heart constricted with fear and confusion as the hound led us closer and closer to the edge of town—straight toward Aelwyn's old Victorian. Rhys didn't speak a word, but I saw his jaw tense up as we neared. I held my breath when the driveway came into view, but the creature didn't turn and instead streaked right past, finally turning in almost half a mile later and sprinting straight for the little cottage that belonged to Fred and Betsy, Aelwyn's closest neighbors. Very human neighbors—which meant they didn't stand a chance against something like a hellhound.

"Shit," Rhys swore as we pulled to a quick stop in their yard.

I didn't answer. The hound had already disappeared inside, passing straight through the closed front door. I jumped out of the truck and sprinted across the yard in pursuit. Rhys was right beside me.

Fred and Betsy were retired. No kids. Not a very active social life. Fred liked to garden. Betsy liked to can. They made preserves for us every Christmas, but that was about as far as my knowledge of them went. If they were in danger now because of some tattoo I'd done—

A hand on my arm yanked me sideways. I let Rhys drag me along, surprised by his strength, until we were both tucked around the corner of the house.

"What the hell are you doing?" he whispered. "You can't just march in there. If that hellhound is being used for something violent—"

"It's my creation, Rhys. My fault. If they're in there, I have to help them."

"Fine, but be smart about it." He pulled a knife from somewhere inside his coat. Its pointed tip gleamed in the dim light.

Silently, I eyed it, then him, and he blew out a breath. "I go first," he said.

I nodded, ignoring the flashback to three years ago. Another night. Another husband and wife. A heart squeezed and squeezed until it just stopped. Tonight's spell might be even worse, considering the sharp teeth on the monster in there.

Rhys crept toward the door, and I stayed close, listening and watching as a light breeze ruffled through the bare branches overhead. It was cold, but it was still—the kind of stillness that always seemed to accompany a freeze. It was also the kind of stillness that made every little noise sound even louder. I forced my breathing to go quiet, taking in a long, deep breath to help steady my pulse.

Ahead of me, Rhys climbed the steps and tried the knob. It turned easily in his hand. The door swung open. I held my breath, still close on his heels as we crept silently inside. A rustling sounded from somewhere in the back. Rhys adjusted direction and headed toward it.

On my arm, Ethan stirred. I was about to let him loose when something squished underneath my boot.

I looked down and cringed at the pool of blood. No, not a pool. A trail. I followed it with my eyes until it disappeared around the corner of the kitchen. Not the kitchen again. Rhys and I exchanged a glance. Somehow he managed to look both concerned for me and violent at the same time. My chest ached for him, but I ignored it and instead focused on the magic that was tugging at me. The magic I'd created and that had called me here tonight.

With slow steps, we made our way around the corner and into the tiny galley kitchen. I stared at the blood on the floor in confusion.

"There's no one here," I said finally.

Rhys bent low, studying the pool of blood more closely now. I stepped around him, caught up in the scene before me as I edged closer and closer. Beside me, Rhys was careful not to touch anything, but by the time I remembered to pay attention, my boots had already wandered too close. When I backed away, I left a set of bloody prints in my wake.

"Damn it," I muttered.

The rustling came again, this time from just outside the back door.

Rhys jumped up, brandishing the knife as he leapt clear of the pooled blood and threw open the back door. I made the same jump, peering around his shoulder just in time to see the two hellhounds merge into one another and become a single solid form.

The hound looked up from where it had bent low over a pile of leaves on one side of the yard, its snout and jaw covered in blood. Fangs protruded from its open mouth, and yellow eyes glowed as it glared down at whatever lay before it. Black fur covered its giant body, and long claws extended from its huge paws. When it spotted us, it gave a sharp howl and then turned for the woods.

I hissed, knowing we were about to lose it for good. Rhys fumbled in his jacket, hopefully for a weapon, but we were out of time. Without stopping to think, I let Ethan peel himself free through the layers of my clothes and coat. He tore free from my skin faster than he'd ever done before, and with a single flap of his powerful wings, he swooped across the yard and dug his claws into the hind parts of the four-legged creature. The hellhound cried out and tried twisting away, but Ethan held fast, and they both jerked sideways as Ethan pecked and clawed at the thing.

I looked back to where the hound had been crouching. Two forms lay half-covered in leaves. I peered closer, unsure of what I was seeing, but after willing my eyes to adjust to the darkness, two faces came into focus. Wrinkled with age and coated in blood, Fred and Betsy stared upward, both of their stark expressions frozen in lifeless terror. I let out a strangled gasp and took a step toward them, but Rhys stopped me with a hand around my waist.

"I see them," I choked, desperation clawing its way up my throat. "I have to help."

"It's too late," he said in a rough voice.

In the distance, a siren wailed.

Rhys and I locked eyes. "Motherfu—" Rhys began.

Ethan screeched sharply.

I swung my gaze back to him as he went flailing and hit the ground several feet away from the hound. I sucked in a sharp breath, every single thought vanishing at the sight of my familiar in danger. I wrenched free from Rhys and ran for my hawk, kicking up a spray of mud in my wake. I was vaguely aware of the hound's howl and its new track—aimed right for me. But I didn't care. I couldn't stop. I had to save Ethan no matter what else happened.

The sirens grew louder, drowning out the sound of my own cry and Rhys yelling my name. For a moment, everything faded, and all I saw was Ethan shuffling toward me in the half-melted snow. Sounds faded.

When I was a foot away, I called up every ounce of magic inside me and sped up. When I collided with Ethan, instead of slamming into me or bouncing off, he melted into a thin layer of magic and ink, and by the time I blinked again, he was nothing more than an image on my arm.

Safe.

He was safe.

Already, I could feel him gathering his energy and healing himself to become the whole creature I'd spelled when I'd created him.

I sank to my knees, gasping for breath and thanking whatever forces had helped me salvage at least one life from this night.

Behind me, something growled.

My stomach tightened as reality came crashing down around me. The hellhound.

I twisted in time to see it lurch for me, its bloody jowls open and sharpened teeth aimed for my face. I screamed.

Over the hound's head, I watched as Rhys sprinted for me. In mid-stride, he flicked his wrist, a quick back and forth that was nearly too fast to follow. Silver glinted through the air. A second later, the knife he'd held a moment ago buried itself in the back of the hound's head. The creature let out a yelp that ended abruptly, and then it fell less than a foot from where I sat, unmoving against the leaves.

Rhys rushed over, yanking me to my feet. I leaned on him, letting him hold me tightly against his chest, stunned by how fast Rhys had moved. How ruthless and true his aim had been and how little he seemed affected by it all. Had he always been able to do that? How had I missed it? What else was he hiding? I started to ask, but the siren reached a crescendo and tires rolled over gravel.

Rhys stiffened and then grabbed my shoulders, peering down at me. "Are you hurt?"

I shook my head. "No, but Betsy and Fred—"

"There's nothing we can do now. Gwen, listen to me. Your footprints are all over that kitchen. It won't look good." My stomach tightened as understanding dawned. Had this been a setup? If so, I'd walked right into it. From the look on his face, Rhys knew it too. His mouth tightened at the edges. "Can you run?"

I nodded. "Yes."

"Do not go to Aelwyn's. Run a mile west past the falls. There's a rock peak there. Do you know it?"

"At the base of Mt. Alexa. Yes, I—"

"Wait for me there. Hide yourself and do not make a sound. Use your familiar to guard yourself. Do not come out for anyone else," he said quietly. "Do you understand?"

"Yes."

He pressed a cold kiss to my forehead, then my lips, but the pressure was gone before I could react. He shoved me toward the trees as a car door opened and closed out front.

"Go," he insisted.

I didn't question his order. Instead, I turned and ran, letting the forest swallow me up, leaving the murdering magic I'd created behind me once again.

CHAPTER 9

*H*uddled inside the alcove of a large outcropping of rocks, I shivered for an hour before Ethan alerted me through our bond that someone was coming up the dirt road. A moment later, headlights came into view. I tensed, ready to run if necessary. Park Ranger Rusty Higgins patrolled the woods around town every night, although he should have been in wolf form instead of driving. I'd been lucky to avoid him so far, and I couldn't afford to be found by him now. Rhys had said he would come, and I had no doubt he would keep his promise, but in the meantime, I was exposed. Cold. Without a single form of defense if whoever was doing all this found me first. I had no doubt now that someone out there was trying to screw with me. Not kill me. They could have done that already. No, instead they wanted to ruin me first. And so far, they were doing a damned good job of it, too.

The headlights swung sideways as a truck pulled into the visitor lot down the hill from where I'd hidden. The base of the great falls was a popular hiking meetup for tourists and even locals. Not at two in the morning, though.

The headlights swung away, and I finally got a look at the vehicle from my vantage point. A sigh escaped me, interrupted by the shuddering of my body. Ethan swooped low enough that Rhys ducked as he got out. It seemed I wasn't the only impatient one out here tonight.

"Gwen?" Rhys called quietly as he started up the hill.

I pushed to my feet and slid out into the open. Rhys breathed out when he spotted me, his shoulders relaxing as he closed the distance between us and gathered me into his arms.

"I was so damn worried. Are you all right?" he asked, wrapping his arms around me and rubbing hard.

Some of my shivering subsided. "I'm okay," I said in a voice that was nowhere near convincing.

"Come on. Let's get you warm and safe."

I didn't argue as he led the way back to the truck. In fact, I didn't say a word as he tucked me inside, spreading a blanket over me before blasting the heat as high as it would go. I sat back to let him shut the door, but he paused, brow creasing.

"Your hawk . . . I'd like to leave him up there for a while to help scout our way. Is that okay?"

Ethan practically screamed at me mentally, and I nodded, a wry smile tipping one side of my numbed lips. "I think you two are on the same side."

"Good." Rhys shut the door and walked around, climbing inside. When he reached across the space and grabbed me, I jumped. He ignored that as he slid me across the bench seat until my thigh was pressed tightly against his.

"What are you doing?" I asked, though I didn't protest the contact. I already felt warmer than I had before.

"Warming you up for one thing," he said, tucking the blanket carefully around me. "And doing a little to help restore my own sanity."

"What are you talking about?"

"I was out of my mind for the last hour," he admitted. "Terrified I'd get here and you'd be gone . . . or worse."

"Did you find Walter?" I asked.

"No, I didn't see anyone else, and the cops are . . . there'll be a full investigation."

I nodded, still too numbed to think too hard about that.

"I don't understand why Walter would have wanted to use his tattoo on innocent people," Rhys said.

"He's not exactly the world's most cheerful person," I admitted.

Rhys shook his head. "Still. Why get it in the first place? A hellhound is a pretty aggressive choice, right?"

I shrugged. "He said he was worried about his safety on the job. He worked for Waste Management and said he frequently had to outrun aggressive dogs and that he'd once stumbled on a bear digging through someone's trash."

"Yeah, I guess I could see that," Rhys said.

We were silent for a minute. "Maybe it was someone else," I said quietly.

Rhys turned to me so quickly, I knew he'd been considering the same thing. "You think someone else activated it? Is that even possible?"

I didn't know what to think, but that didn't change the fact that the hellhound had been here and done some real harm. "Sure, I mean, with the right magic, anything's possible, right?" I shrugged. "All I know is someone wanted to hurt innocent humans and they used my tattoo to do it. Again."

Rhys bit his lip. "Gwen, we're going to figure this out. It's going to be okay."

I nodded, my eyes stinging with tears. "Rhys, I . . . Thank you."

"For what?" he asked.

"For all of it. Protecting me and caring for Aelwyn and for saving my life tonight. I'm sorry I've been so selfish when you— I should have thought more about your feelings in all of it. I should have realized everything you gave up just to keep me safe."

"I'm sorry I walked away, Gwen. It's the single biggest regret of my life." His voice was hoarse with emotion, and I felt my own eyes sting as I blinked back hot tears. "You're the most important thing in the world. Making you happy is all I've ever wanted."

I swallowed hard as he stared down at me, aware of our closeness. And suddenly it wasn't all about warmth or worry. His chest heaved, and I leaned closer, my body straining for more of him. The air around us thickened, and the world outside faded. There was only this—the two of us. And how badly I wanted him to kiss me.

"Gwen," he whispered, his gaze dropping to my mouth.

Like a mind reader, he lowered his head, his lips brushing over mine in a feathery kiss. I sighed, and my reaction spurred a growl from deep in his throat. His lips crashed over mine, suddenly demanding and desperate. I threw off the blanket and wrapped my arms around his neck, holding him as close as I could and willing this moment not to end.

His hard chest pressed against my own, his breath washing over me and doing more to warm me than any blanket so far. But it wasn't enough. I needed to be closer. After all this time, the reality was so much better than I ever imagined.

I grabbed his shoulders and shoved him back, climbing onto his lap with my knees digging into the seat belt holster and the armrest along the door. Rhys held my hips tightly, helping me adjust as I settled on top of him. His mouth never left mine, and when I lowered my center to his, he pressed against me, his tongue shoving against mine until I moaned softly.

I felt Rhys harden against his jeans.

My hands tangled in his hair, pulling and pleading for more.

He kissed me like we were drowning, but it was the opposite. This was the first moment I'd felt like breathing in three years.

"Wait."

I tried not to feel a pang of disappointment and fear when Rhys eased back. He squeezed his eyes shut and dropped his head, and I braced myself for the rejection that was about to come. But when he opened his eyes, a smile tugged at his lips. "You are ridiculously sexy, you know that?"

"I . . ." I blinked.

"We need to get you somewhere safe before we can . . . finish this. But we will finish this. I just . . . Protecting you comes first, okay?"

"Okay," I said shakily.

He held onto me as I slid back to my seat, tugging me close again when I ventured too far. I waited while he readjusted the blanket, tucking it in around my legs—and then adjusted himself. When he looked up, I sent him a small smile of my own at my handiwork. He responded by planting a quick kiss on my mouth before straightening and backing us out of the empty lot.

Neither of us spoke on the ride back to town, but Rhys held my hand tightly the entire way. I was sure I'd have more to say when I was warm and coherent again. For now, the silence felt nice. Rhys's hand in mine felt even better. Right here, I was completely safe. I just hoped it would last.

CHAPTER 10

*B*y the time we arrived at Rhys's apartment, I was ready to burst with questions. Between making out with Rhys and the truck's heat, the cold had been chased away, and the fog had lifted. My thoughts were clear—and overwhelming. I had too many questions to know where to begin. And the grief of seeing Fred and Betsy like that . . . I tried not to blame myself, but it was hard. The biggest question, though, was Walter.

The Dirty Knuckle was empty and dark when we pulled around back. Rhys showed me inside and up the back stairs, unlocking the door and then stepping back to let me go first. I walked cautiously. My eyesight was sharp enough to keep me from running into things, but my slow steps had nothing to do with that. This was Rhys Graywalk's private space. And I was standing here with the scent of his body still on my skin. It was a lot —even with the whole nearly dying thing, it was a lot.

My heart thudded extra hard as I stood in the center of the living room and waited while Rhys went around turning on lights. He disappeared around a corner, and I heard cabinet doors and then a fridge. A moment later, he returned with two dark bottles already opened.

"Drink this," he said. "It'll calm your nerves while we talk."

I took the beer gratefully and sipped, mostly to keep from having to talk. I didn't know what to say about the apartment. It was all dark wood and leather, like his office. But it was lived in. A sweatshirt thrown over the arm of the couch. A newspaper and stack of magazines spread over the coffee table. Dirty socks by the door. It was so personal. I didn't want to admit how many times I'd ached for him to bring me here over the past few years.

So I drank until the moment passed.

Rhys downed half his beer and then set it aside. He strode to a rolltop desk in the corner of the room, slid it open, and pulled out a pad of paper and a pen. He returned to where I stood and tugged me down on the couch beside him.

"Okay," he said, the pen poised and ready, "tell me what else you know about this Walter guy."

"First tell me what happened after I left the house." Fred and Betsy's. That's what I would have normally said. But saying their name now . . . I couldn't.

Rhys frowned, but nodded. "It was a setup, that's for damned sure. Deputy Conall said he got an anonymous call to come check out a disturbance, but no one else even lives close enough to be disturbed, even with the racket that beast made. So that doesn't add up. And the blood in the kitchen—that was a message."

"You think whoever unleashed the hellhound was the same person that killed Aelwyn?"

Rhys nodded. "I do. And I think they wanted us to know that, too. I didn't have much time to look over the bodies before Conall chased me off, but I think whoever left that blood in the kitchen did it before the hellhound got there. And the energy signature was the same as the one at Aelwyn's that night."

"Ethan didn't sense anyone else out there with us," I agreed. "So they must have already left when we got there."

"Ethan?" Rhys blinked.

"My hawk."

Rhys stared at me, brows raised. "You named him Ethan?"

"Yeah."

"Ethan Hawk?" He laughed out loud, and my lips curved at my own private joke. Aelwyn had been the only other person who knew, so I'd almost forgotten the humor of it.

"It was Aelwyn's idea," I admitted.

He smiled warmly. "Sounds like her."

My smile vanished too quickly as I remembered what we were doing here in the first place. "Do you think . . . I mean, whoever killed her is messing with me now. Do you think they killed her to get to me?"

Rhys took a deep breath. "Honest truth? I do. And I'm sorry. For what it's worth, I managed to wipe out your footprints in the kitchen, so they failed tonight."

"Failed?" I felt the blood drain from my face. "Fred and Betsy are dead because of me. Because of my tattoo. That's not a fail, that's—"

"I know. Bad word choice. I'm sorry. Gwen, how do you know Walter couldn't have activated his tattoo?"

"Because I check up on him. On all of the ones who have magic in their ink. After last time, I realized I had a responsibility."

"Last time wasn't your fault."

"That couple would still be alive if it weren't for me."

"Gwen, that asshole was going to hurt his wife with or without your help. The tattoo was a heart, for goodness' sake. There was no way you could have known he'd find a way to twist that into violence."

"You're right. He could have done something different, but he didn't. And then his death—"

"Was his own damned fault. He should have come out and surrendered when the police told him to. Instead, he ignored their warnings and shut himself in that house. If not for him, she could have gotten medical attention in time. He let her die and then let himself get shot when they stormed the house. None of that is on you."

His voice was firm and almost angry now. Aelwyn used to talk to me about it the same way. They wanted to assure me. But my own guilt was so much bigger than their ability to convince me I wasn't to blame.

"I know that," I said, but we both knew I didn't. Not really.

Rhys sighed. Finally, he spoke again, changing the subject. "So you know for a fact Walter couldn't have activated that hound."

"Yes."

"Hmm."

"What?" I studied his face as a shadow passed over his features.

"That means someone else knows about your gift and how to activate the magic. Is that possible to do on someone else's ink?"

"I've never tried, so I'm not sure. What are you thinking?"

"I just . . . Conall showing up tonight was weird. I want to check on that anonymous call. Verify it really happened."

"You think Deputy Conall is the one doing this?"

"I don't know. But he seems all too eager to point fingers at you for Aelwyn. Besides, we don't exactly have a long list of possible suspects."

I hesitated and then said, "Well, there's one."

"Who?"

"Ada."

"Ada Daryn?" His eyes narrowed. "What makes you think she would do this?"

"She's been blackmailing me into giving enchanted tattoos," I admitted.

"Gwen, what the . . . Why didn't you say anything?"

He didn't sound nearly as surprised as I'd expected. I cocked my head. "Something tells me there's not much to tell."

His mouth tightened, and he set the pen and paper aside. "I've seen her coming and going from your place."

"You've seen her?" I repeated, my eyes widening. "Have you been watching me?"

"I'm your Protector, Gwen. I have to keep an eye. But since . . . I've kept my distance for a while now. I knew you didn't want me to come around, so I stayed out of sight. But I had a job to do, and I wasn't going to let anything happen to you just because we weren't—" He broke off, and my temper flared.

"Because we weren't speaking," I finished for him. "You mean because you rejected me?"

He winced. "Don't say it like that."

"How else should I say it? That's what happened, Rhys." I waited for the hot fury that usually rose when I thought about his rejection. But this time, all I felt was sadness. His apologies were getting to me, and I could feel myself edging closer to giving in to his pretty words. But the fear of being hurt twice hadn't gone away entirely.

"Gwen." Rhys grabbed my hand and squeezed. I turned to meet his eyes, and my stomach flipped just like it always did when his gaze turned so intense. "I hate that I did that to you. I never should have let it go this long. But the oath—"

"I know," I said. "You already explained. I just . . . it's a lot to let go of." Too much, maybe. But I didn't say that.

He nodded and then pressed a kiss to my lips. His mouth was warm, a solid comfort after everything that had happened tonight. I kissed him back lightly, expecting him to stop it just like he had in the truck. And I couldn't blame him. We did have a killer to catch. Besides that, I wasn't sure what this was yet. I'd wanted it for so long, but now that I had it, I had no idea how to process it against the years of thinking he didn't want me.

But he slid closer, reaching for me and pulling me swiftly into his lap, his tongue exploring my mouth and leaving my skin prickling where his fingers trailed.

"Rhys . . ." I whispered against his mouth.

He responded by pulling me closer, his hands roaming everywhere before slipping underneath my shirt. I panted against him, arching into his palm as he cupped my breast.

Outside, a hawk called sharply, and we both went still.

My shoulders sagged as Rhys eased me away. He rose and went to the window. I followed reluctantly, adjusting my shirt and bra and then running a hand through my hair, which was probably already a nightmare.

"Is he okay?" Rhys asked, throwing the window open and peering out into the night sky.

"He's fine," I said wryly, bracing myself against the gust of cold air that blew in. "Just letting us know it's all clear."

Rhys turned back to me, his confusion melting into amusement. "He can sense us . . .? I mean, he knew we were . . ."

"He's my familiar. I see through his eyes, and sometimes he sees through mine."

"I see." Rhys smiled mischievously. "No pun intended."

"Funny."

"You should call him back before the sun comes up," Rhys said, and I nodded, knowing he was right, but wishing Ethan had kept his mouth shut for a while longer. I still wasn't entirely ready to trust Rhys, but I couldn't deny how badly I wanted to try.

"And when the sun does come up?" I asked, already sticking my arm out the window to call Ethan back to me.

"We'll pay a visit to a friend at the Court," he said. "See what we can uncover about Ada. And the deputy. And figure out where to look next." He turned and began building a fire in the cold hearth near the couch.

I called Ethan back to me and then sank onto the soft couch as the fire crackled to life. We sat in silence for a few minutes, finishing our beers. When mine was empty, I leaned my head back against the soft leather. Between the warmth of the flames and the crackle of the wood, I couldn't keep my eyes open.

Soon, I drifted.

I woke to the jostle of being lifted by a pair of strong arms. When I opened my eyes and saw Rhys staring down at me in the firelight, I protested against his firm grip. "I can walk," I insisted.

"You looked so peaceful. And tired," he said quietly. The firelight danced strangely over his features. "Let me carry you."

Struck by the hard planes and strong lines, I looked away and let him carry me to the spare room without further argument. He tucked me into bed with gentle hands that contradicted his sharp edges, and didn't help the pitter-patter of my traitor heart. When he was gone, I tried not to register the disappointment that he hadn't carried me to his bed instead.

I woke to the smell of coffee and the sense that I wasn't alone. When I rolled over, my breath caught, and I gasped. Rhys jumped back, nearly spilling the coffee he'd just set on the nightstand. I blew out a breath, clutching my chest and willing my pulse to steady as I sat up. "Shit. You scared me."

"Sorry. I wanted to offer caffeine before I started overloading you with information."

"What time is it?" I asked, inching toward the steaming mug and trying to blink the rest of the exhaustion away.

"Almost ten."

"In the morning?" I squawked.

Rhys winced. "My contact called me back a few minutes ago, and I think we should meet with a couple of people today. I didn't want to wait too long to get moving."

"Why? Who? What did he say?" I grabbed the mug and took a sip, mostly so I could comprehend whatever details he was about to give.

Rhys hesitated. "Take another sip of coffee first."

"Rhys," I warned, irritable and wary. "Tell me."

He didn't respond, and finally I took a large gulp of coffee. Then I raised my brows. "Now tell me," I said.

"They found Walter's body this morning."

"What?" It was the last thing I'd expected, and for that reason, it confused me more than upset me. For about five seconds. Then my eyes stung with tears that I blinked back. In an effort to hold it together, I gulped more coffee. "How did he die?"

"Natural causes. That's the official finding so far. But . . ."

"We both know it wasn't natural. Not with the hellhound getting loose."

Rhys' brow furrowed. "Is it possible his tattoo could have activated when he died?"

"No. The magic only lives as long as the wearer."

He let out a breath, but he didn't look relieved.

"What?" I asked.

"Remember the call Deputy Conall claimed to get about the disturbance last night?" I nodded. "My contact says Walter was the anonymous caller."

"That doesn't make sense. Walter let his hellhound loose and aimed it at innocent people he likely didn't even know, and then he called the police?"

"It doesn't make sense," Rhys agreed, his gaze far away as he stared at the curtains covering the sunlit window. Finally, he blinked and looked at me, focusing on my body for what felt like the first time since he'd come in.

Suddenly, I remembered I'd taken off everything but my black tank top and panties last night. My exposed skin tingled where his gaze touched.

"I should get dressed," I said hastily, reaching for the sheet, coffee still clutched in one hand, but Rhys stopped me. Carefully, he took the mug out of my hand and set it on the nightstand. Then he scooted closer until we were almost nose to nose. His eyes blazed with a hunger that I'd only ever experienced in my own body. Desire—no, need—reflected back at me.

Slowly, he reached for me, his hand cupped tightly against the back of my neck, his thumb stroking my jawline. He held me there, his expression daring me to object.

"If you think for one second that I'm done with you," he said, and then rather than finish that statement with words, he kissed me.

The second his mouth met mine, heat exploded inside me. His kiss wasn't gentle or soft or anything resembling asking my permission—not like it had been last night in the truck. Instead, he took, his mouth hot and heavy, his hands demanding as they explored. And damn if I didn't let him.

Screw enchanted tattoos—this right here was the real magic.

His hands roamed my body, down my arms and then over my hips, all while pressing into me with his mouth and his erection. My skin thrummed where his fingers touched—my collarbone, my throat, tangling in my hair. He leaned against me, easing us both down so that I was on my back against the bed and Rhys was pressed against me in all the right places. My blood heated, and I rocked my hips against his, lost in the feel of him. Of knowing he wanted me. Finally.

My left hip tingled extra hard, but I ignored it, too caught up in the moment to do anything but appreciate my body's reaction.

When his tongue darted inside my mouth and tangled with my own, I clutched at his shirt, fisting my hands in the fabric in desperation. His hand dropped from my hair long enough to hook behind my knee, drawing my leg up and wrapping it around his waist. He rocked into me, and I lost it, my head falling back against the pillow as Rhys pressed a trail of hot kisses down my throat before nipping at my ear. His fingers found the edge of my panties, and my insides sizzled in anticipation as his hand slipped inside the thin fabric, inching toward my center.

It was everything I'd wanted for so long.

Without warning, Rhys broke off, his eyes wide, his mouth open in a shocked expression.

"What the hell?" he demanded, jumping clear of me and the bed in one leap.

Iron clanged against iron as the tattoo that had peeled itself away from my hip took shape, color, and then dimension, and finally fastened itself to Rhys's body. He stared down at it, dumbstruck as it welded itself together—tight from the looks of it. Painfully tight.

Dazed, I stared up at where he stood with his back to the bedroom door. It took a moment for the fog to clear and the tingling to subside enough for me to notice what was happening. When I finally did, I had to press my lips together to keep from laughing. The twinge in my hip suddenly made sense. After all this time, I'd almost forgotten.

Rhys glared back at me, indignation hard to accomplish in his current state. But he managed. "What the fuck is this?" he demanded.

"Um, I believe it's called a chastity belt," I supplied, sitting up so I could get a better look at my own creation.

"Are you kidding me?"

I decided not to answer, fairly certain anything I said would unleash the laughter I was holding back. Rhys glared at me, the iron clanking as he shifted his weight. "You did this—your tattoo . . . Why the hell would you do this?"

"I honestly forgot about it," I told him, guilt creeping in as I watched him struggle to unlock the thing.

His eyes narrowed, clearly unconvinced.

I tilted my head as the memory returned. "That day in my backyard when we were— The day we first kissed . . . I was hurt when you broke it off and walked away."

"I hurt you, I get that, but a chastity belt, Gwen?"

I shook my head, caught up in the memory that had scarred me so deeply that I'd inked this protection into my skin to keep it from ever happening again. "I was nearly naked, and you just stopped. Then you walked away and left me there, Rhys. Standing there like an idiot. That was right around the time of my Awakening, and I was starting to understand how my ability worked. So, I inked myself with a defense mechanism. If you ever tried anything with me again, it would activate the spell behind the tattoo and, well, this would happen . . . Thus, saving me from you."

"What about last night?"

"Last night was a kiss. This was . . ." I felt my cheeks heat. "About to be more."

He stared at me. "If it's to keep you safe from me, shouldn't you be the one wearing it?"

I folded my arms over my chest, smiling haughtily. "Why should I be punished if you were the one who started it?"

He shook his head, muttering to himself. I caught enough of it to glare back at him, but the sight of him saying anything while standing before me trapped in a medieval chastity belt was too amusing. Before long, I was biting back more laughter.

"I bet you think this is funny," he said, taking a step closer so that the iron clanged again.

A small laugh escaped. "It's pretty hilarious," I admitted.

He stepped even closer, sending me back against the headboard as he sat so close that he crowded me. His brows had dipped so that his expression was serious, intense. I couldn't quite read whether he was still pissed, but the heat in my stomach was curling again.

"You're only laughing because you haven't really thought this through," he said, his voice dropping low as he leaned in.

"Oh?" I blinked, trying to stay focused on what he was saying rather than how hot he looked while saying it.

"If I'm all locked away, it's going to make the outcome pretty frustrating for you." His hand came up to cup my breast, and I bit my lip against the moan that built. His voice dropped to a whisper, his lips grazing my chin as his fingers found my nipple and tugged slightly. "Especially when I'm touching you like this . . . Don't you think?"

Damn it. He was good.

With a sigh and a small flick of my wrist, the iron vanished.

The second the iron was gone, Rhys sighed in relief. "You're more diabolical than I ever knew, you know that?"

"Now you know why I don't walk around inking everyone with this sort of magic," I said.

"Damn right." He shuddered. "I'm terrified to imagine what the hell is going to happen to me when we actually have sex."

My lips curved just as his mouth covered mine.

CHAPTER 11

*C*upids & Cuties, the annual celebration that always took over Havenwood Falls, was three days away, and the evidence was all over town. I didn't necessarily hate Valentine's Day. Hating it would have required giving a shit in some way, which I didn't. Normally, I had no problem ignoring the whole thing, though I did roll my eyes at the cliché hearts and cupids I ended up tattooing on couples this time of year. Still, I couldn't hate on a holiday—or a town event—that was so good for business.

This year was different, though.

Business was already booming, thanks to the herbs wearing off. And Rhys Graywalk was currently walking next to me—a simple thing that made my heart race and my palms sweat. He was also eyeing the pink and red décor currently coating the town square.

"Wow, that's a lot of pink," he said.

"Ugh. It's stupid is what it is."

We'd had to park around the corner thanks to all the service vehicles delivering décor for the square. I wove through the swarm of them on our way from Rhys' truck to my apartment. As if it wasn't weird enough that Rhys Graywalk was about to see where I lived, now we had to navigate there through an entire herd of cardboard cupids being carried by delivery workers who wouldn't stop smiling at me and offering a hello.

My life had become really fucking weird.

"When you say 'stupid' are you referring to Cupids & Cuties?" Rhys asked, increasing his pace to keep up with me. "Or the entire concept of Valentine's Day?"

"All of it, yes, but mostly the event itself. The idea that an enchanted arrow can lead you to your true love and when it does, you have to kiss the person right there in front of a ballroom full of people? It's bullshit."

"Spoken like a true Grinch."

I caught his teasing grin and scowled as I turned to climb the steps that led to the shop. "Are you saying you're a fan?" I asked, suddenly nervous that he'd tell me he'd been there every year and made out with a different girl each time.

But he shook his head. "Actually, I've never been." He bumped my shoulder. "I had a feeling the arrow wouldn't work without you there, so I've always skipped it."

My face heated, but I ducked my head, grumbling to cover up my pleasure at his words. "Well, I think love takes a lot more work to find than an enchanted arrow."

"Can't disagree there."

At the top of the stairs, I unlocked the door of my shop and headed inside. I didn't stop in the dark shop, but kept walking straight through to the next set of stairs that led up to my apartment. "You can just wait down here if you want," I said, not bothering to look back in case it gave away just how nervous I was to have Rhys in my living quarters.

But his footsteps didn't slow or stop, and his voice came from close behind me as I shoved open the door at the top of the steps. "No way. I'm not letting you out of my sight after last night."

I bit back a quick retort, mostly because I didn't want to ruin the agreement I'd managed to get out of him at all. I'd had a hell of a time convincing him to let me come here in the first place. And part of me would have been happy to stay away until all this was resolved, but I couldn't afford not to be here when my first client showed. Not with the packed schedule I had thanks to the herbs wearing off and the people in this town actually wanting to be around me. Rhys had argued, but I'd convinced him to give me ten minutes. Not eleven. Ten. That was it. The plan was to grab a few things, reschedule all my appointments for the next couple of days, and get out again. Fast.

It should have been more than enough, but then I stepped through my front door, and the energy signature in my tiny one-bedroom hit me. It was fae, but it wasn't mine.

I took a quick step back, but Rhys was even faster, grabbing me by the waist and yanking me behind him. I huddled behind him, my heart pounding. Rhys didn't move a muscle as we both listened.

Outside, there was a thud, and my head whipped to the window. Rhys bolted, beating me there, and together we peered at the street below. I caught sight of a man's shoulders and head just before the figure's feet hit the ground. Once he'd landed, he looked up at us, and it took me a moment to register what I was seeing.

Walter Glass stood staring up at us from where he'd just swung himself down two floors using the rafters and railings. The only thing different about him from the last time I'd seen him, other than the fact that he was supposed to be dead, were his eyes. The brown color had changed to a bright yellow, glowing to an impossible hue before dimming again. He blinked, and the yellow vanished, replaced once again by the dull brown that I remembered.

"Impossible," I said, but even as I breathed the word, his eyes flashed with fury, and a ripple of magic passed over his face. It was only a split second, but it was enough, and I realized why we hadn't been able to identify the signature before.

"It's a glamour," Rhys said flatly.

I didn't argue. I knew Rhys had received this particular gift during his Awakening, and now he could see through any fae's glamour, Seelie or Unseelie, no matter how old or powerful.

"That's not Walter," I said, the hushed words coming out more like a question.

"No, it's a fae glamoured to look like Walter. It's also the same energy signature I sensed at Aelwyn's. And again last night," Rhys added. His voice was quiet now, like a simmering rage that he was keeping under tight control.

"Can you see his face?" I asked. "Do you recognize him?"

"Yes. I've never seen him before, but his markings suggest he's an Unseelie soldier of some kind."

"Seriously?" How in the hell would an Unseelie soldier get into Havenwood Falls unchecked?

Dead Walter stared up at us, and the full weight of the glamour resettled over his features before he took off at a full sprint. Rhys moved to follow, then stopped just short of the window that led to the fire escape.

"Why aren't you going after him?" I asked.

He didn't look up as he slid his phone out and started typing. "We need to know more about who and what we're dealing with first."

He had a good point, but still, letting a dead man run off through town didn't seem like the smartest play. I eyed Rhys warily as he keyed in a few lines and sent a message. "You want to call the police?"

"Yes, but first, I want to reach out to my police contact to see if he can dig up anything else on Dead Walter. Then we'll go see someone at the Court. Maybe one of them can tell us anything about that glamour we just saw."

"And in the meantime?" I asked, already impatient as he set his phone aside and leaned against the counter.

"We wait."

"I thought you said we weren't safe here."

"We're safer than roaming the streets until we know more. If Walter wanted a fight here, he could have had it—and the element of surprise. Instead, he ran. I think we should lay low here until we know what our next move is."

"Fine." I sighed, resigning myself to sitting around for a bit when all I wanted to do was run outside and chase Walter down.

"Tell me about Walter's other tattoos."

"Walter doesn't have any other tattoos," I said slowly.

Rhys looked over at me. "Well, Dead Walter does, but they have a lot more magic in them then that hellhound did."

I frowned at that. If Dead Walter was really an Unseelie fae, and he was covered in magical tattoos that I certainly hadn't given him, that meant I wasn't the only one with this ability.

"Do you think he found my mother?" I asked. "That he made her give him those tattoos?"

"No."

He sounded so sure.

"How do you know?" I asked. "If he already has magic tattoos, he had to get them somewhere."

"If something had happened to your mother, I would have heard, trust me. Besides, if he wants you badly enough to risk coming here, glamoured or not, it means he needs your gift. It means he doesn't have it already. I think those tattoos were done by witch-magic. They felt different than yours."

"Different how? What did they look like?" I asked.

"I only saw one of them clearly. It was an azurite stone." He hit send and slid his phone away again before responding. "Azurite is a divination stone. It would . . . possibly allow him to see past the shields you have. To find you—if he knew what or who he was looking for."

"What shields?" I asked.

"The mistletoe." He nodded to the room around us. "And the cedar wood."

"The cedar wood's a shield?" That was news to me. Then again, hadn't that letter from my birth mother mentioned cedar wood? Most of my furniture had been a gift from Aelwyn, but I didn't think—

"It protects your house. Aelwyn spelled it to work against fae. Especially anyone not from Havenwood Falls."

"Oh." I blinked, stunned.

Rhys' theory made sense. If the azurite tattoo had allowed him to pick up on what I really was, he would have ended up at Aelwyn's for sure. Between her energy and mine, that house was laced with fae magic and enough cedar wood, or shielding, to make it clear we didn't want to be found. I swallowed the lump in my throat, blinking back hot tears as I realized Aelwyn really had died because of me.

Rather than dwell on that here, now, under Rhys' sharp eyes, I forced myself to focus on what Rhys was proposing about the azurite.

"Wait." I blinked. "You think he came through one of the portals? But wouldn't the Court have sensed that?"

"They would. They have," he amended, looking only slightly guilty as he admitted, "I got a text from my contact yesterday morning. There was a breach a few days ago that they still haven't identified."

My eyes widened. "And you were planning on telling me this when exactly?"

He sighed. "It's not like we've had time to really sit down and catch up on every little thing. We started to last night before your tattoo alarm system went off."

I stalked to the chair beside my sagging couch. "Point taken. Let's go ahead and do that now."

"Gwen . . ." Rhys looked tired despite the fact that it wasn't even lunchtime yet. I couldn't blame him. We were both night owls, and I couldn't remember the last time I'd been up before brunch.

"You wanted me to come to you for help, Rhys. And you told me that whole story last night about you being a Protector and where I really come from because you wanted me to trust you. Why ruin it now by keeping things from me?"

He shook his head. "I'm not hiding anything from you, Gwen. There's a lot happening here, and I'm trying to keep up and keep you alive."

I sighed. "You're right. Sorry, I'm just stressed."

"I know. Just . . . take your herbs," he said, and I pushed to my feet. "We'll start there. Get the shields back in place so people don't see you so easily."

I winced, and his eyes widened. "Shit, I'm sorry. That came out wrong. You know what I mean."

"It's fine." I waved him off and turned toward the kitchen, where I kept my herbal supplements.

"It's not fine," he said, following me. "You're scared, and you're counting on me, and I don't mean to insult you."

"I . . ." What could I say? I *was* counting on him, but I wasn't ready to admit that out loud. "I'd like to find a way to be of use in this whole thing," I admitted instead.

"You will," he said, with enough certainty I decided not to admit how much I doubted that right now. "Your magic is strong, Gwen. More than enough to stop this guy from taking it or from hurting you." He stepped closer, grabbing my hand with his own and spinning me to face him. "I believe in you."

He barely applied pressure, but the contact alone was enough to halt me in place. I turned slowly and met his eyes, the look he gave going straight to my stomach. Butterflies flipped and flitted inside me. And the heat that curled there shot low, straight to my thighs. "Rhys," I began.

He stepped closer, and I remembered the way he'd felt pressed against me when we'd first arrived. Not to mention kissing in his truck last night. And earlier this morning. The heat inside me seemed to warm the space between us, charging the air with a spark. Without consciously deciding to, I curled my fingers tighter around his, willing the moment to last. Suddenly, sitting and waiting for our next move didn't seem so bad.

Rhys bowed his head, leaning in, and I held my breath. Every single thought of the danger and the uncertainty vanished. All that mattered was this moment.

A small voice deep down warned me against getting distracted right now. And Ethan scratched at my arm, reminding me of the very real danger we were both in until we found answers to why a dead man had been inside my apartment. But none of it penetrated the fog of my own desire. And for a moment, neither did the insistent buzzing of a phone that broke the silence between us.

The buzzing continued, and Rhys sighed, his breath warm as it washed over my face.

When he pulled away, I came crashing back to reality. We did not have time for this right now. Not with a glamoured fae on the loose and out to get me.

Rhys pulled out his phone, checking the screen before looking back at me, apology written all over his expression as he stepped away.

"It's my contact at the Court," he explained. "We need to go. Now."

CHAPTER 12

From the cab of the truck, Rhys frowned as we both studied the empty spaces where tattoos had once covered my side and hip. The hellhound had left a large blank spot on the right, and then the chastity belt had disappeared on the left. Then there was the missing heart from where it had lived for a short time on my chest. It was strange seeing so much smooth, unmarked skin when the rest of me was practically covered in ink. Guilt pricked at me for the hound. And even more so for the heart. Not so much for the belt. Rhys had definitely deserved that one.

"So they can only be used once, right?" Rhys asked, even though I'd already explained it all. Twice.

"Right," I said, exhausted.

The light ahead turned green, and Rhys hit the gas. He hadn't told me yet where we were going, and he'd already turned away from the Court's headquarters in town. But he was also keeping me talking, which made it hard to wonder too much about it.

"So the hellhound," Rhys said as he made a right turn. "What would have happened to it if we hadn't killed it?"

"I'm not exactly sure. I mean, when the spell had run its course, it would have vanished. Its only power lies in executing its order. But . . ."

"It had already killed Fred and Betsy, and it was still coming after you," he finished for me.

"I've never seen that before," I admitted. "Unless the spell was more complicated than we thought."

"What do you mean?" Rhys pulled to a stop at a four-way intersection. When it was clear, he went straight through. This part of town was mostly industrial. I wasn't sure where we could possibly be meeting a Court member in this area, but he pulled into a half-empty warehouse lot, wound around behind a row of buildings, and cut the engine.

"Well, the words used to activate it are simple. It's all about the intention of the person wearing it. If his intention was to have it kill Fred and Betsy, it should have blinked out. But . . ." I trailed off, unwilling to say the words out loud.

"But if it's intention was to, say, pin a murder-suicide on you, it would still be kicking when we arrived," Rhys said grimly.

"Yeah." My voice was hoarse.

For a moment, we were both quiet as we digested this new theory.

"Gwen, we have to report this to the Court."

My head snapped up, my gaze whipping to his. "What? How can you ask that of me? I'll be arrested or banished."

Rhys shook his head. "I can speak for you. I—"

"What the hell good would that do? The facts are all there. My tattoos have helped kill four people so far. There's nothing you could say."

He growled. "If you'd just told me about the magic, that it wasn't over with that one tattoo, I could have helped you."

Touchy. We were both touchy as we forced ourselves to dance around the issues between us. My issue was that we had a killer to find, and all I wanted to do was make out with him on the couch like a high schooler. I sort of hoped that was his issue, too.

I huffed. "And whose fault is it that we weren't on speaking terms all this time?" He opened his mouth. Closed it again. "And don't act like you didn't know. You were watching me, remember? You know more than I probably want you to know right now."

"It was my job, Gwen."

He was right. And his job had kept me and Aelwyn alive and safe until now. I couldn't bring myself to keep arguing.

I sighed. "To answer your question, yes. The magical tattoos I give can only be used once. As soon as the magic has run its course, my copy merges with theirs, and they both disappear forever," I explained.

"But Ethan is different," he said.

"Yes." I hesitated. I'd never actually told anyone any of this. Except for Aelwyn. And she was gone. "Ethan is . . . I realized a couple of years ago, that if I want to, I can create something more permanent."

"But you've never done that with the spelled tattoos," he said.

I shook my head. "It only works on myself anyway."

He grunted. "Thank the gods you didn't decide to do it with that damned chastity belt."

I smirked.

"Does anyone else know about Ethan? About the permanent aspect?"

"Just Aelwyn," I said quietly.

Rhys didn't answer, but his expression was thoughtful and dark.

"What?" I prompted.

"I think it's obvious our guy is using your tattoos to get to you. He won't come directly at you, though. And I think we need to try to figure out why. It could be that he knows about your true ability. That he feels you're enough of a threat to play it careful."

I nodded. "But what is his end game? What does he really want from me?"

"I don't know yet." Rhys yanked the key out of the ignition and reached for his door handle. "Come on. Let's go inside and see if we can find some answers."

He got out of the truck, and I followed, looking around at the nondescript building. No signage or markers were displayed. The handful of buildings in this area served as mostly storage facilities for local business and delivery companies. I couldn't understand who or what could possibly help us here.

"What are we doing here?" I asked.

"Meeting a friend," he said. I gave him a pointed look at his vague answer, and he sighed. "A friend who works for the Court."

I scowled up at the two-story building where it rose in front of us, blocking the sunlight. "If that's true, I don't have any friends in there."

Rhys ignored that, trudging on ahead toward the door.

In the end, I followed. Maybe I didn't have any friends on the Court, but if Rhys did, it couldn't hurt to try to get them on my side. Especially when Ada came sniffing around again for another piece of ink and found me all closed up.

Inside, I stayed close as we wound our way through the halls. No one else was around, though I could hear machinery running somewhere deeper in the building. Rhys seemed to know where he was headed, and I wasn't about to tell him differently, so I let him lead. Ten minutes later, we'd found a receptionist of sorts. A tall, broad-shouldered man with white hair and black, leather gloves greeted us with a simple nod before herding us into a small conference room with a scarred table and four wooden chairs. No windows. No other equipment.

Rhys immediately sat, stretching his legs out and slinging his arm over the adjacent chair. Relaxed. I might have paced if there had been room. "Relax, Gwen. No one is going to mess with you."

I spun, irritated that he'd read me so easily. "Easy for you to say," I muttered. "That guy looked more like a hit man than a secretary."

Rhys smiled in amusement. "He's neither. Calm down. He's just a driver."

"A driver for whom?"

Before Rhys could answer, the door opened, and an old man with silver hair strode in. My muscles tensed as recognition dawned. I'd seen him before, always at a distance. Aelwyn hadn't been close with him, though she'd visited with him from time to time over the years, and she'd always described him as stern, so I'd steered clear. But this close, I could feel the aura around him that spoke of his age. Elsmed Fairchild was a member of the Court. He was also the oldest living fae I'd ever met. And between my own blurred line with the law and those piercing blue eyes he now fixed on me, he was intimidating as hell.

"Miss Facharro," he said in a clipped and vaguely polite tone. He gestured to a chair. "Please. Sit. Rhys, good to see you, son."

I lifted a brow at Rhys and sat.

"Good to see you too, sir," Rhys said, leaning forward and folding his hands together on the scuffed tabletop.

Elsmed sat too, somehow folding his long body into the small chair. I wondered at the way he let more of his true height show. Way too tall to pass for human. Did he add glamour only when he was out in public? Or was he only letting it all show now to scare me on purpose?

If so, it was working.

If Rhys had asked me the member of the Court I least wanted to be put in a room with, it would have been Elsmed. The man was rumored to have a gift for mind reading. And that was the last thing I needed now. My eyes narrowed as I recalled Rhys imploring me to be honest today.

Was this why? Because he knew I'd have no choice but to admit what I'd done.

My mouth went dry.

"Your messages said you had new information about Aelwyn's case," Elsmed said.

Rhys nodded.

"Tell me what you know," Elsmed said.

I shot Rhys a look, absolutely not okay with sharing everything with a man that, for all I knew, was the fae behind the attacks. But Rhys ignored me, clearly more trusting of this guy, and began laying it all out. "We know Aelwyn was killed by a fae. So were Fred and Betsy."

"Do you have proof of this? What do the police say?" Elsmed asked.

"No physical proof," Rhys admitted. "But the energy signature was the same at both houses, and today, I saw a dead Havenwood Falls resident leaping from Gwen's apartment window. He was glamoured and underneath I saw the markings of an Unseelie soldier."

"You saw him?" Elsmed said, much more interested now.

"Yes. He escaped as Gwen and I entered, but I saw through his glamour, and he is definitely Unseelie fae."

"Hmm. And this dead resident," Elsmed said, glancing at me. "You knew him?"

"I tattooed him a while back," I said, nodding.

"So Gwen is at the center of this after all," Elsmed said to Rhys.

Rhys nodded with a grimace. The truth wasn't exactly good news. "Aelwyn was killed moments before Gwen arrived. I don't think that was a coincidence."

"You think they wanted to torture her? Make sure she found Aelwyn as it happened?" Elsmed asked.

Rhys nodded. "And maybe pin it on her. That much was clear at Fred and Betsy's."

Elsmed frowned. "I wasn't aware Gwen was present at the second scene. The police report didn't mention her."

Rhys shot me a glance, but pretended not to notice the death stare I was giving him as he continued. "She left before the police showed up. I . . . thought it best until we can gather a list of viable suspects."

To my surprise, Elsmed nodded, rubbing his chin thoughtfully. "I can't disagree. The sheriff seems to have tunnel vision here."

"He has his head up his ass," I muttered.

Elsmed's gaze swung my way, and I wished I hadn't let that slip. "What do you think this person wants from you, Gwen?"

That silenced me. I debated my answer—partly out of genuine speculation. And partly out of self-preservation.

When I didn't answer, Elsmed nodded knowingly. "I realize you have no reason to trust me," he said. "For what it's worth, Aelwyn was a dear friend to me, though in recent years we kept our distance for . . . various reasons." Something about the way he said that caught my attention. "Rhys has kept in close touch, letting me know how your family is doing and whether you need anything that I can provide. I want to help you, whether you can believe that or not, but in order to do that, you will have to be honest with me."

"I . . . What reasons?" I demanded.

Elsmed blinked.

"Trust goes both ways." I lifted my chin. "What were the reasons that kept you from Aelwyn?"

"Gwen," Rhys warned.

Elsmed lifted a hand and waved him off. "Valid question and fair point." He looked at me, studying. "You were the reason, Gwen. We wanted no contact or interference with fae for your own safety. So I kept my distance. We didn't want someone using me to get to you. I'm too high profile in this town to ignore that possibility. And as I said before, I do want to help you."

I chewed my lip, debating. Finally, I blew out a breath. "They want my magic."

Elsmed gave no visible reaction to that, which only made my anxiety worse. "Your fae magic?" he asked.

I nodded, swallowed hard, and then answered. "My tattoos," I said, gesturing to the ink peeking out from the collar of my shirt. "They . . . I can make them come to life. Some people have used them for violence, so I don't offer the service up anymore, but . . ."

"Someone has discovered your talent anyway," he finished. I nodded. "And they are using it against you with these murders?"

Rhys shook his head. "Aelwyn's death wasn't magical—"

"Except that they knew about the mistletoe and the cedar wood wards," I pointed out.

"And Fred and Betsy?" Elsmed asked.

"A hellhound," I said quietly. "I inked it a couple of years back."

"And do you remember the person who purchased that tattoo from you?" Elsmed asked.

Purchased. He made it sound like nothing more than buying a sweater. I snorted.

Rhys was the one who answered. When he did, his voice was grim. "It was Walter Glass. The deceased Seelie fae I mentioned earlier."

"He's the one who ran from Gwen's apartment," Elsmed said. "The glamoured Unseelie soldier?"

"Yes," Rhys said.

The room fell silent.

"I see," Elsmed said finally. He looked at Rhys. "So we know that a dark fae is here to exploit Gwen's gifts."

"How do you know he's dark?" I asked sharply.

"Because the signature on the portal shows an unauthorized fae entry," Rhys explained. "And no Seelie fae would glamour themselves to look like a dead guy in order to go unnoticed."

I scowled, but said nothing. I knew the whole light and dark argument when it came to fae. I also knew most of them lived up to their reputations, thanks to the Unseelie apprentice I'd taken on last year. But I wasn't a fan of prejudgment based on one's genes. Then again, the guy that had killed Aelwyn, and maybe even Walter, was Unseelie, so maybe it was that simple after all.

"Hmm. But we also know he doesn't want to kill her. At least not yet," Elsmed said.

I shuddered at the casual tone he used to talk about someone trying to murder me.

"And we know this dark fae can glamour himself to look like anyone he chooses," Rhys added.

"Yes, but so far, he's only appeared as the dead," I said. Both men looked at me, and I went on. "So far, he's appeared as Walter who was already dead at the time—and I think . . ." My forehead crinkled as I thought back. "The day after Aelwyn was— I was there going through her things, and I saw something out the window. It was only a split second, but it looked so much like her. It was enough to startle me, and by the time I got outside, they were gone."

Rhys just stared at me.

"What?" I demanded irritably. "You're not the only one withholding information."

Elsmed's lips twitched. "Interesting. Well, that does present a problem, either way."

"It's going to make him damn near impossible to catch," Rhys agreed. "If Gwen won't hand over her gift—"

"He'll just take it," I finished for him, my voice hushed with horror.

Elsmed nodded somberly. "My guess is he needs you alive in order to soak up what you have to offer. That's why he continues to lure you out. He needs to get you alone long enough to steal your magic. He can't kill you until that's done."

Rhys huffed. "The question is, what can we do to identify him? I can sense his energy signature, but I can't penetrate his glamour enough to recognize his face."

Elsmed rubbed his jaw. "The Court is working with the police already on the portal breach. What you've learned about his ability to disguise himself will be valuable toward that. I can put the word out—"

"We can't go through the Court," I cut in.

"Do you have something against justice?" Elsmed asked, one brow rising in challenge.

I could feel Rhys's eyes on me, probably a glare that was meant to shut me up, but I purposely ignored him. "Considering I'm the prime suspect in my own mother's murder, I don't see how justice has much to do with it."

Elsmed considered me for a moment and then threw a glance at Rhys. "She makes a fair point." Before I could say anything else, he added, "But since revealing this new information would remove you from the suspect list, I'm assuming you're mostly just worried about Ada's preoccupation with your ability."

I gaped at him and then tried to cover it with forced innocence. "I don't know what you're—"

"Gwen, your secret is safe here, in this room." He cocked his head. "And just to reassure you, I have no intention of using your gifts for my own gain."

I just stared at him, at a loss. Apparently, the rumors about Elsmed being some sort of mind reader were true. Judging from the surprised look Rhys wore, he hadn't betrayed me. Elsmed had to have picked all that out of my mind—I'd been thinking about it hard enough since we'd arrived.

"It's not an exact science, you know," he said—again, reading my thoughts. "But you do make it easy."

"I . . ." I had no idea what to say to any of that, but I forced my back straighter, heart pounding.

"Your gift is incredible," he added.

No intonation. No clue if that was a good thing or a death sentence.

"It's dangerous," I corrected. "And not something I want becoming public knowledge."

"I've kept your secret for twenty-two years already. I have no intention of revealing it now."

Really?

"Sir, I'd like permission to put Gwen into protective custody," Rhys said, and my head snapped up.

"Wait. What?" I demanded.

"I can't say I disagree," Elsmed said slowly.

Rhys looked relieved.

"Now just hold on, damn it." My temper flared. "I'm right here. You don't have to talk about me like I'm not in the room. Or like I don't get a vote."

"Unfortunately," Elsmed went on like I hadn't spoken, "the police are diverting all of their resources to their ongoing investigations."

"Diverted where?" Rhys asked.

"The Bennett case, for one. Not to mention the ongoing investigation into Aelwyn's death and the unauthorized portal use we're still looking into."

"I think it's pretty clear all these things are connected," Rhys said.

"While that is probably true, between these and a few internal matters, we simply don't have the manpower to assign an official protective detail at this time."

"I have a friend I can call," Rhys said.

Elsmed tilted his head as if listening into the silence, then his eyes lit. "Gargoyles?" he asked, and Rhys nodded.

"I'll call Everett before we leave," Rhys said. "He can have two of them here in a couple of hours or less."

I was a little surprised at how easily Elsmed accepted that Rhys was taking matters into his own hands. Clearly, this wasn't the first time he and Rhys had worked together. I considered arguing about the protective detail, but knowing there were others watching out for me did make me feel better right now.

Elsmed turned to me. "I do recommend you resume your herbal supplements."

"My . . ." The mistletoe and the cedar wood. "You knew about that?"

"I was the one who suggested it," he said.

"But my mother gave those instructions before she sent me here from Faerie."

"Exactly."

My jaw opened. "You were there? When I was sent here?"

"I've had an eye on you for a long time, Gwen. You are very special and important to your people."

My people. He spoke as if they belonged to me. Or I to them. Like I should have felt a connection somehow. But how could I connect with a people I'd never even met?

"Funny. I don't feel very special. Or important."

"That's because Havenwood Falls is about equality. Blending in. Many of our citizens come here to get off the radar. The ones who are on it don't particularly like the sort of attention that comes with it."

"When this is all over, I'd very much like to visit Faerie," I said. The words were out before I'd thought much about them. But as they settled in the space between us, I knew I'd meant them. Without Aelwyn, I had nothing tying me here. There was Rhys, but . . . I didn't want to think about how complicated that felt just now. Or how uncertain.

Elsmed nodded. "Take a few days. Lay low. Stay with Rhys. We're doing all we can to look into the portal and the deaths. The wards in this town won't allow an intruder to go undetected for long, glamoured or not. Once this is resolved, we'll discuss your trip."

He rose, and Rhys did the same. Finally, I did too, thoughts racing at the idea that I might get to see where I came from. More importantly, I would get to meet my mother.

Elsmed opened the door and stood just outside in the hall. A clear signal this meeting was over.

Rhys nodded at the elder as he passed through, heading back the way we'd come with heavy steps. I moved to do the same, but Elsmed stopped me, bending close.

"The hellhound was quite the creation, you know."

I went still. Again, trying to decipher his true meaning. "I . . . It's awful the way it was used," I said.

"True. Still . . . very creative. And impressive."

"Thank you?" I couldn't help that it came out like a question. No one had ever complimented me like this before. Like it was a gift rather than a curse. Like I should be proud.

"Don't worry. She won't bother you much longer," he added, and I blinked, hope blossoming immediately.

"How do you know?" I asked, too desperate for answers to care too much about implicating myself any further.

He patted my arm before dipping his head and striding off, his steps completely silent against the stained hardwood. His driver-slash-secretary fell into line behind him. I stared after them, hoping like hell he was right.

CHAPTER 13

I slammed the cabinet doors, stomping around the kitchen as I eavesdropped on Rhys' phone call with Sheriff Kasun. I didn't even know what I was looking for, exactly; something to take the edge off, maybe. When I finally settled on a beer and a bag of chips and stomped out again, I found Rhys leaning against the doorframe, watching me. He offered a small smile as he tossed his phone on the narrow breakfast bar.

"What did that cabinet ever do to you?" he joked.

I scowled and shoved past him, flopping onto his leather couch.

Behind me, I heard the fridge open and close. A moment later, Rhys joined me on the couch with a drink of his own. It dawned on me then how rude I'd just been to help myself to his alcohol and not offer him one, too. I sighed, cracked my beer, and reminded myself I was a guest here. And Rhys was actually trying to help me. He didn't deserve my temper.

"Sorry," I muttered, and since I didn't say the word often, it grated on me. "I just want to strangle the sheriff for not taking this seriously."

Rhys took a long drink and nodded. "I can't disagree about the strangling part. But they're doing what they can on the investigation."

Elsmed had warned us the police wouldn't share any information on the case, but Rhys had tried anyway, hoping for a different answer. No such luck.

"I heard the conversation just now," I admitted.

"Then you heard Kasun explain they can't comment on an ongoing investigation."

I pinned him with a look. "Why do you think I'm irritated? Come to think of it, why aren't you irritated?"

"Simple." Rhys shrugged. "If Kasun isn't willing to comment, it means you're not the only suspect. It means they're actually looking into this from all angles. Following all leads. It means they're going to help us catch this guy."

"Or I am the suspect and he knows that puts you guys on opposite sides," I pointed out.

"Kasun doesn't know what I am to you," Rhys said.

"Oh." I sat back, unsure what to say. Did I know what Rhys was to me? Did he?

We drank in silence for a moment. Our earlier meeting with Elsmed Fairchild played on a loop in my mind—especially his promise at the end to take care of Ada for me. If he managed to do that, I wouldn't have to give any more magical tattoos. Maybe ever. Just the thought of it made my shoulders a little less heavy. That and knowing two gargoyles had arrived to sit outside and keep an eye out for glamoured fae.

"She would be proud of you, you know."

The words jarred me, yanking me out of my hopeful daydreams of a very boring life as a very normal tattoo artist. I blinked up and found Rhys watching me closely. His words sank in slowly, and my chest ached as I thought of her. Aelwyn.

"I don't know. She was always pushing me to embrace the magic. To find a different side, to see it as a blessing instead of a curse." I shook my head. "If she were here now, she'd probably just lecture me some more about having faith in the universe or something."

"You don't?" he prompted.

"What?"

"Have faith?"

"I have faith that what you put out comes back. And that there are a lot of bad people in the world—and more of them seem to be drawn to my gift than anyone good." I couldn't help the bitterness that coated that last word.

"You expect bad things to happen to you."

I shrugged. "Expect the worst, hope for the best."

Rhys looked away, his face falling and his expression clouding over into something unreadable. I swallowed hard, not sure why I was suddenly struck with the urge to comfort him.

"I hate that," he said finally, his voice raw and coarse in the silence.

"What—" I began, but he shocked me into silence by getting up and coming to sit beside me on the couch. He set his beer aside and folded his leg, sitting sideways so he could face me. His knee jutted gently against my thigh, and my leg tingled at the small contact.

"It's my fault. For shutting you out and making it hard for you to trust people. I'm so sorry for that. I hope you can forgive me, Gwen. I hope . . . Aelwyn would want us to be there for each other."

My stomach tightened. "So all of this . . ." I waved my hand around at his living room. "It's for her?"

"What? No. Of course not."

"Because you weren't going to tell me the truth about yourself otherwise, were you?"

"Gwen, I—"

"How long are your orders for?"

He sat back. "What do you mean?"

"Your oath to protect me," I said. "Will it end when this threat is over? Or will it continue?"

"I have sworn to protect you for as long as you are alive," he said, and the way he said the words sent tingles down my spine.

"And are there . . . rules about getting involved with me? Will you get in trouble if we . . .?"

"No trouble," he said softly. "But there is one rule."

"What is it?" I asked, not even sure I wanted to know based on the intense expression he wore.

Gently, Rhys took the bag of chips and set both it and my drink on the coffee table. Then he scooted in again.

He took a deep breath before he spoke. "Once we're together, we can never break up. It's all or nothing for Protectors. Our choice has to be final."

"Oh." I licked my lips, not quite daring to tell him that's how it already was for me.

His eyes burned into mine. "That's why I stopped our kiss and walked away from you before. What I felt for you was so deep, and I knew what would happen if we continued. I knew there would be no going back for me, and I couldn't let that happen without you fully understanding what you were getting into."

"What do you mean?" I asked. "What would have happened?"

"My soul would have forged a connection with yours, and that's not something I can break," he admitted. "You would have been trapped."

I blinked, staring into his dark eyes, searching to be sure he was serious. "Oh," I said again. I was so smooth.

"I understand if you need to think about it now. Take all the time—"

"I don't need to think about it," I said quickly, then blew out a breath. "Sorry, I guess this is unexpected. I didn't think you'd ever . . ." I searched for words that hopefully wouldn't sound as awkward as they did in my head. "Rhys, you've had my heart since the moment I saw you."

He scooted closer. "You have no idea how long I've wanted to hear you say that."

"Yes, I do," I said, the words no louder than a whisper. "Because I've wanted it all along too." My heart thudded wildly, and I swallowed hard against the nerves I felt admitting all of it aloud, but he'd already apologized—more than once—and made it clear how he felt about me. All while I'd thrown it back in his face. And for what? To punish him? Except all it did was punish me, too. And I was tired of doing that. If Rhys was offering himself up, I was going to take him. Rhys was my Protector, but he was also my one and only love.

"I'm sorry for being so angry all the time," I said.

"You had a right," he began, but I shook my head.

"I use anger to cover my hurt so that people can't really see me, but all that does is make the pain worse. I want you to see the real me, Rhys."

"Gwen, you have to know how sorry I am about hurting you before." His voice was rough with emotion. "But I couldn't risk breaking my oath, and I had to protect you first and foremost. That kiss . . ." He trailed off, his expression twisting into regret.

"It's in the past." I reached for his face and ran a hand down his stubbled cheek. "I loved you when I was six and I love you now, Rhys Graywalk. You are my choice, always."

His lips spread into a slow smile that lit his eyes. "I love you, too, Gwen Facharro. I always have, and I always will."

Slowly, he reached out and let his fingers trail down my cheek and around my neck. The air around us felt tense, like the universe was just waiting for us to make the next move.

Rhys leaned in. His lips brushed over mine, and just that soft, quick contact was enough to make me tremble. I squeezed my hands together, praying he hadn't noticed the way my arms shook at his touch. But then I opened my eyes and caught sight of his wary expression. My eyes widened. "What's wrong?"

"I just want to make absolutely sure," he said uncertainly.

"Sure of what?" I asked, but he was eyeing my arms, his glance skittering over my torso and up to the ink that peeked out from underneath the collar of my shirt. "What are you doing?" I asked when he reached for the hem of my shirt and yanked it up, scanning the tattoos covering my abdomen and hips.

"After the chastity belt incident, I'm not taking any more chances," he said, frowning as he inspected my skin. "I need to know if you have any more magic ink up your sleeve." He grinned up at me, still holding my shirt up. "No pun intended."

"Hilarious," I said, yanking my shirt down again. "And no, you're safe."

The wariness turned to a calculating gleam full of mischief. This was a side of Rhys I hadn't seen in ages. "Am I now?"

I leaned away, cocking my head as he crawled closer, forcing me back until I was lying flat and he hovered over me. The romantic moment had vanished, but in its place was a playfulness I'd missed.

"Well, I don't know about safe. But nothing is going to attack you if you kiss me," I said.

He grinned, his teeth flashing at me just before his lips feathered across my own. "That's too bad," he said, lowering his body to mine. He paused long enough to wink as he added, "I've always secretly hoped it would be you doing the attacking in the end."

I wasn't one to disappoint.

CHAPTER 14

A buzzing sound stirred me from sleep. The following *thud* jolted me awake. I looked around, half panicked until I realized the sound was just a cell phone vibrating with an incoming call. Rhys looked up at me from the floor, where he'd rolled off the couch thanks to our still-entwined ankles. He blinked dazedly before reaching for his phone on the coffee table. I sat up and ran a hand through my tangled hair as I struggled to get my bearings. It was early—too early for sunlight judging from the darkness that framed the edges of the closed blinds. I tried to remember how we'd both ended up tangled and half-naked on the couch. Empty beer bottles littered the coffee table along with cartons of rice and noodles.

Last night came crashing back to me in a renewed wave of heat, leaving my body tingling as I remembered the way it had felt with Rhys pressed against me, bared skin to bared skin.

"Yeah." Rhys greeted whoever was on the other end in a gravelly voice that drew my eyes to his. He stared back at me as he listened, his dark hair wild from sleep. His hand reached for my arm and stroked lazily—until he suddenly stopped moving, all of his attention focused on the caller. "Are you shitting me?"

I glanced up from where my gaze had wandered down his bare chest. He frowned, the expression sending his brows furrowing. He listened for another moment and then grunted a goodbye before hanging up and tossing the phone back to the coffee table. It slid and bumped a Napoli's takeout container before coming to a stop.

"Who was that?" I asked.

"Emile. The bar manager," he said, and judging by his tone, I knew that wasn't a good thing. He rose, fumbling through the pile of clothes on the floor and picking out his jeans. He tugged them on quickly, which only made me more alert.

"He was calling you now?" I asked.

"He just locked up and left. Late night," he added, when my eyes widened as I noted the time.

"What did he say?"

"He found something outside he thought we should see."

Before I could ask what it was, there was a sharp knock on the apartment door. Rhys jumped up, his jeans slung low on his hips as he padded down the hall. I listened as the front door to the apartment opened. Low voices rumbled, too quiet for me to make out more than a few words.

"Thanks, man," I heard Rhys say before the door clicked shut.

A second later, he reappeared, a manila folder in hand. His expression was tight, and my stomach clenched at what could possibly be inside.

I waited while Rhys opened the flap and pulled out a handful of photos, fanning them out on his lap. My chest tightened, and my stomach dropped straight to my knees. I went still, staring at the photos as Rhys picked up each one and examined it for a long moment.

"This asshole's a real piece of work," he muttered.

I couldn't believe he was so calm about it all. But then, it wasn't his future on the line here. And maybe that made less of an impact somehow.

I could only stare, openmouthed and speechless, as Rhys flipped through them all. A candid of me standing in Aelwyn's backyard the night she died, Ethan peeling away from my skin, half-inked and half-formed as he took flight. Another of the hellhound, a shimmering, translucent monster, passing through the door of Rhys's truck as it led us on the chase. And a third—this one showing Rhys and me locked in a heated kiss with me straddling him in the cab of his truck.

All of them were invasive and threatening in a different way. And all of them made it clear that whoever had taken them knew my deepest secrets. Not just my gift for ink, but my feelings. Rhys. They knew about Rhys. And the message was clear: they could get to me, to him, anytime they wanted. One way or another, eventually, they were going to hurt me.

"I think I'm going to be sick." I clutched my stomach, willing it to settle against the churning panic. I rose, pacing and shoving a hand through my hair over and over again.

"Calm down, Gwen. He's just trying to intimidate you—"

"Well, it's working!"

Rhys frowned.

I blew out a breath. "He knows my secret, Rhys." I gestured to the photo of Ethan. "He knows what I can do."

"That's why we have to show these to Sheriff Kasun."

"Are you kidding? Hell, no. Forget the sheriff. If he sees these, I'll be a suspect of totally different crimes. We need to handle this ourselves."

"Gwen, they need to know who we're—"

"You show them those photos and the first thing they'll do is lock me up."

"Elsmed then."

I hesitated, part of me wanting to resist even that. But I nodded, knowing I had to give him something. "Fine."

"I'll make the call." He was already grabbing his phone from the coffee table as he spoke.

I stood stiffly, watching Rhys move as he punched in things on his phone. I noticed his glamour tattoo inked onto his right shoulder and went still.

"Rhys, what's your tattoo?" I asked, sharply enough that he looked up from the phone.

"An arrow," he said. "Why?"

I licked my lips, thoughts whirring. Arrows. My weapon of choice. Rhys liked knives, but I could do that too. And rope—to bind him. And—

"Gwen?" Rhys wandered closer, his eyes studying me, his brows knitting at my silence. "If you're upset, don't be. I got it for you. For your love of archery and because it reminded me when I came here that I needed to stay focused on my target—"

"I'm not upset," I said. "I just . . ."

"Gwen, what is it?"

I hesitated, wondering whether I was being too impulsive or reckless. That maybe I should stand back and let Rhys ask Elsmed for help. Hide inside this apartment and wait for the Court to find this guy and take him out. But the reality was that whatever semblance of personal safety I'd had had vanished the moment I'd seen those photos. Even inside this apartment, we were just waiting for this guy to decide he was ready. It was all on his terms, and I hated that most of all.

Fear held me back. Rhys believed in me. In my ability to use my own magic to defeat this guy. But could I really? My mother thought so, I realized, remembering the letter.

When the time comes, she will not have to hide. They will hide from her.

"I don't know yet. I need a second to think," I said slowly. I bit my lip, adding, "I have an idea but . . . Go make your call and then we can talk about it."

"Okay," he said uncertainly, but he backed off and went about sending the message he'd been typing. A moment later, his phone buzzed with an incoming call.

I waited while Rhys spoke to Elsmed or his bodyguard-slash-driver, thinking again about that arrow tattoo. I had no idea if my plan would work, but I did know that making a damned phone call was not enough. It was time to take action. It was time to finish this once and for all. On our terms. And I finally knew a way to do it.

CHAPTER 15

$\mathcal{I}$ was lost in a sea of ghostly masks, and for a split second, I couldn't breathe at the sight of all the people filling the ballroom at Whisper Falls Inn. Coming to the party was a huge risk—which was sort of the point. It was also grating on my rebellion against every commercial thing about this stupid holiday. And to top it off, I'd somehow been convinced to wear a formal dress. "For the mission," Rhys had insisted. "To really sell this we have to blend in," he'd added. I'd shot back that if we really were doing this for the mission, it meant full sleeves to hide my tattoos and a wig to cover my hair. But even with all that, Rhys had stared at me the entire drive over, and I wondered if his reasons hadn't been more selfish. Either way, we were here now. With any luck, we wouldn't need to stay long.

Beside me, Rhys was silent as he surveyed the crowded room from the entryway. We were what Aelwyn would have called "fashionably late," which meant soft music was already playing from the orchestra in the corner. Couples were already swaying to the song. And well-dressed waiters wandered between milling guests, offering hors d'oeuvres. A familiar face caught my eye—the only face not wearing a full white mask. Our hostess, Michaela Petran, was fast approaching us. She wore a forced smile wide enough I thought her face would crack.

"Gwen Facharro, holy shit! I can't believe you're here! And Rhys. So glad you guys could make it. Nice to see you two together." She added more emphasis on the last word than was necessary, but I didn't argue.

"Thanks for having us," Rhys said, a lot less enthusiastically than Michaela. "What do we need to do, exactly?"

"Well, first off, you both need masks." She thrust white masks at each of us, still grinning.

"And why is that, exactly?" I asked.

Rhys shot me a scowl. I knew I shouldn't question this. It was one of the reasons we'd chosen this venue to lure our dark fae out of hiding—the masks. The anonymity. But I couldn't go quietly, apparently.

"Love goes beyond what we can see on the outside," Michaela explained. "Cupid's aim strikes at the heart—that's how you know it's true love."

I did my best to hold in the snort. I didn't disagree with the sentiment; true love was about much more than looks. But the idea that these silly arrows could help someone find their soul mate was such a gimmick. Everyone knew love spells weren't real.

"Got it," I mumbled.

Rhys stayed silent.

We each took our masks and slid them on. I adjusted mine carefully so that I could see out of the tiny eye-holes, but the visibility wasn't great. My muscles tensed as I realized spotting our guy before he attacked was going to be even harder without peripheral vision.

"And here are your arrows." Michaela held out two white arrows trimmed in gold, one for each of us.

Rhys grabbed his and nodded at Michaela. "Thanks."

I took mine gingerly. Michaela smiled at that and winked. "When their aim is true, they'll light up for you. Follow the arrow's tip to your special lover's lips."

I blinked. Was she for real?

Rhys shifted. "Um, thanks."

Michaela herded us inside. "Happy kissing," she called as we walked off.

I decided to pretend I hadn't heard her. She was becoming more and more like her old bubbly high-school self, whom I'd never been a fan of.

Rhys let me lead the way, and I wove through the guests toward the bar at the far end of the room. If I had to be here, I needed a stiff drink, that was for sure. Skirts swished at my feet, and people in masks murmured hellos as we weaved in and out of the bodies. Rhys stayed close on my heels, and I knew he was nervous about the anonymity. But it was the best idea we'd had, and Elsmed had actually endorsed it when I'd insisted on pitching it to him last night. In fact, he had assured us he'd have a security team stationed around the room, too, including two gargoyles I'd never met, but who made excellent protectors, according to Rhys. And, of course, Michaela had been alerted that there was a possibility of an arrest tonight. She didn't know we were involved, and I was glad for that. I'd hate to be the one to ruin her party. From the looks of it, she'd put a lot of effort into this night, her first big event since taking over the inn.

If I thought the town square had been lavish, this was opulent. White roses were everywhere. In the centerpieces for the standing tables, draped from the stage, and hovering above us along the walls, held in place by some sort of magic—or really strong duct tape. And carefully placed among all the white were pops of red. Roses, silks, and even mixed in among the glassware, everywhere I looked, the red grabbed at me. It was supposed to be classy romance, I was sure. But it reminded me too much of the blood dripping from my hands as I'd kneeled over Aelwyn's body.

"Gwen?"

I blinked, snapping back to the party as if the whole thing had reappeared out of thin air. Rhys was waiting, and I wracked my brain, trying to recall what he'd just said. "Um, wine?"

It was, thankfully, the right answer.

Rhys nodded and turned back to the bartender. I scanned the room, forcing myself to breathe evenly and focus on the moment at hand. Elsmed promised his men would be here, but so far, no one was standing out as possible undercover agent. Everyone seemed to be here for drinks and kisses—and there were plenty of both to go around.

I thought of the weapons we'd smuggled inside—several of them worn in the form of fresh ink against our skin—and hoped they would be enough. Or that our dark fae would show up at all. Maybe kissing strangers wasn't his thing.

We got our drinks and then wandered to the edge of the room. I felt a lot better with my back against the wall, and I suspected Rhys would too.

"Do you think he'll come?" I asked, facing the crowd, constantly searching the anonymous faces for some sign of our killer.

"I think if he does, we'll be ready for him," Rhys said quietly. I'd been amazed at the sheer amount of knives he'd managed to attach and conceal on his body before we'd left. How he could walk like that, while still bending his knees, was pretty impressive. Still, I'd seen enough damage left by this guy to be nervous for Rhys. For both of us.

"I thought I'd recognize more people. I thought they'd have their masks off by now," I said, irritated by the lack of recognition for people I'd literally grown up around.

"You just have to look for other markers," Rhys assured me. "See there? The woman with short, silver hair?" He pointed. "That's Jetta Mills. And there? The purple hair? That's Julianna Fairchild."

"Yeah. Okay, that makes sense. I see it now." I forced a deep breath in, then out slowly.

"Look for those clues," Rhys encouraged. "And if you see anything strange, let me know."

For a few minutes, we watched and quietly pointed out when we each recognized someone in the crowd. The sight of the familiar figures made me feel a little better until I remembered our guy could literally be any of them now.

Rhys finished his drink, and a waiter appeared to take his empty glass. I handed him mine, still half-full. I couldn't drink when I was already so tightly wound.

"Don't scratch it," I said quietly when the waiter was gone. "It'll draw attention."

Rhys dropped his hand from where he'd been rubbing at a spot on his arm through his suit jacket. I watched his hand fall to his side and then let my gaze trail up his arms to his chest and back down again. My thoughts wandered to last night; the ink I'd given him and then the part that came after . . .

"Are you checking me out again?"

I jerked my gaze back to his and could just barely make out his eyes through his mask's holes. They were crinkled in silent amusement.

"I'm checking to make sure your bandages haven't leaked through to your shirt," I said stiffly.

"Uh-huh. We both know your ink didn't draw enough blood for that," he said, clearly trying to bait me. "You're too good at what you do."

"Fine. I was checking you out," I admitted, softened by the compliment. "You look pretty nice in a suit."

"You look pretty nice all the time," he shot back. "Especially naked on my couch. But tonight, in that—" He nodded at the white gown I wore. "You look like an angel."

I snorted. "Are you trying to insult me?"

He blinked and then rolled his eyes. "I didn't mean a literal angel. Havenwood Falls has plenty of those. I meant . . . you look hot," he finally finished.

I smiled behind my mask, glad he couldn't see how stupidly large my grin was. "Thanks."

On my right, someone cleared their throat, and I jumped, nearly dropping my arrow.

"Hello," said a male voice, somewhat amused as I tried to breathe through the adrenaline pumping through me.

"Hello," I countered uncertainly.

I didn't recognize the voice, which meant it wasn't Walter—or anyone else I knew. Rhys and I had already discussed this. Our dark fae could still be running around as Walter—but probably not. In fact, chances were he'd already moved on to another glamoured disguise. Especially now that everyone knew Walter was supposed to be dead. He could literally be anyone. Which was exactly why we'd chosen Cupids & Cuties as our backdrop. If he was going to be anonymous, so were we. I just hoped between the masks that hid our faces and our freshly inked tattoos serving as weapons, it would be enough.

"I was just wondering if . . ." The mystery man beside me held up his arrow, pointing it awkwardly at me.

We both waited. Nothing happened.

Finally, he sighed. "Well, it was worth a shot. Have a good night," he said and wandered off, still clutching his unlit arrow.

I looked over at Rhys and found him watching our mystery man with narrowed eyes.

"What?" I asked.

"He thought his arrow might light for you," Rhys said in a strange voice.

"Ridiculous." I huffed.

"Are you referring to the arrow pointing toward true love or the idea that anyone could want you to be theirs?" Rhys asked.

"Take your pick," I muttered.

"Gwen, he's not the first person whose attention you've attracted tonight," Rhys said.

I felt my cheeks heating. "But . . . it's not like any of them talk to me normally."

"You're a little . . . hard to approach when you're not disguised," he pointed out.

I scowled.

"Not to mention the mistletoe you take."

"Point taken."

Rhys continued watching the human mystery man, and I bit my lip, still trying to decipher his strange tone. Was he actually jealous of some human with a spelled arrow? I'd been a little distant since we'd slept together on Rhys's couch. It wasn't so much the sex as what came afterward that had me unsettled. Rhys said he wanted me—not just for today but forever. And goddess knew I wanted him. But with a dark fae killer after me and the future so uncertain, I wasn't sure whether I could let myself believe him just yet. Maybe when all this was over. Maybe then I could really open myself to Rhys and his promises.

I let my thoughts wander, both of us still watching and scanning the guests. But everyone looked like they were supposed to be here. A few arrows lit up here and there, and people giggled or just tore off their masks, smiling—all too happy to lock lips with their other half.

"These arrows are really stupid," I muttered, feeling like a Scrooge more than ever. I wasn't even sure why.

"Really? I think they're kind of nice."

I rolled my eyes, still watching the latest couple to match arrows. They'd removed their masks and pressed their lips together, both of them unconcerned at the room full of onlookers.

"How can you think it's nice? The magic is obviously fake," I scoffed. "It's like a classy orgy that—" I pulled up short as I turned to Rhys, my eyes locked on his arrow. It was lit a bright white. And the point was aimed at me.

When I didn't react, Rhys reached for my arrow and gently spun it in my hand. He set it back against my palm so I was the one holding it, the point aimed at his stomach. Immediately, the entire thing lit up to a bright white.

"Well, shit," I muttered.

Even with the mask, I knew Rhys was grinning as he closed the distance between us. "Looks like we get our own orgy right here in the corner."

"Rhys, we have to stay focused," I began but he'd already ripped his mask aside, leaning toward me, lips puckered. He grabbed the edge of my mask, lifting it just enough to expose my mouth—and pressed his lips to mine.

CHAPTER 16

*V*aguely, I was aware of someone clearing their throat. It took me a moment to come out of the haze of the kiss. When a hand closed over my elbow—and I realized both of Rhys' were wrapped around my hips—I jumped, yanking back and whirling on the third hand. A man stood there, masked and dressed in a tux with a red bow tie. His hair was slicked back, and his skin was pale. A vampire, maybe? His dark eyes were sharp enough as he studied me. I dropped my very human glamour long enough to let my senses read him properly.

I stiffened. A vampire, yes. Not that I was concerned. But he had another scent on him. One I recognized all too well now. The dark fae we were hunting.

Rhys took a step forward so that he was blocking me from the man. I could only guess he'd noticed it too. "Can we help you with something?"

The vamp rolled his eyes, not bothering to react to Rhys or the way he'd drawn up his chest and shoulders.

"Here," the vamp said in a bored voice. He thrust a slip of paper at Rhys and wandered off.

While Rhys unfolded it, my eyes tracked the vamp, but he made a straight line to the door and ducked out of the ballroom. Huh. Someone whose aversion to this party outweighed my own.

Rhys growled, and I snapped back to the note he'd been handed.

"What does it say?" I asked.

"It's from Elsmed. He has new information. Wants us to meet him out back." Rhys didn't move, though.

I bit my lip. "Do you think it's a trap?"

"If it is, that means our guy knows Elsmed is helping us. It also means —I hate to say it, but . . ."

"He could *be* Elsmed by now," I finished.

Rhys grimaced.

"The only thing we know for sure is that he isn't you or me," I said, trying to stay calm even though my heart was threatening to pound right out of my chest.

Suddenly, the partygoers filling the ornate ballroom before us were more threatening than festive. And I wanted nothing more than to be gone from this room.

"Right, but . . ." Rhys trailed off.

"But what?" I asked, because if Rhys was nervous, I was nervous.

He hesitated. "In order to protect ourselves from whatever's waiting out there, the smart thing would be to split up. I go out to meet Elsmed and you—"

"Do not say 'stay behind,'" I warned.

"Actually, I was going to say you should watch my back," he said. "Let's slip into one of the rooms upstairs with a balcony. You can let Ethan loose and watch me from there. If anything looks wrong, you have your tattoos and can help get me out of there."

I mulled that over, but he had a point. Our entire plan tonight had hinged on improvising once we knew where "Walter" was hiding. I'd already assumed part of that would include splitting off to appear weaker to the dark fae we wanted to draw out. So, I couldn't complain about this detour. Well, I could, but it wouldn't do much good.

"Deal," I said.

"Let's go."

I let him take my hand, and together we navigated our way back to the door. Thankfully, Michaela was nowhere to be found, so we didn't have to explain our early exit. In fact, the lobby and stairs were all deserted, and we found our way upstairs without much trouble.

Out on the balcony, Rhys waited while I let Ethan out, and we watched as he took flight, soaring up and out of sight quickly. Then we both stared down at the east side of the inn's property.

Immediately to my right, a third-floor turret rose and I had to lean around it to scan the rest of the lawn. From the balcony's view, the large lawn was bordered by a narrow driveway that led down to a row of cottages on the right. On the other side of the cottages, a line of trees separated the inn's property from the rest of the block.

To my left, the street and shop lights of Main Street sparkled in the distance, reflecting off the snow below, bright enough to see for a long way out.

Even with my fae sight and the brightly-lit night, I couldn't spot Elsmed or anyone else among the trees that lay beyond the property's edge.

"Something moved down there," I said, "But I can't tell who."

"Same here." Rhys turned to me. "If it turns out to be a trap, I want you to—"

"Rhys," I warned sharply. "Don't say something that makes me sound like a damned damsel in distress. If it's a trap, I'm saving your ass. If it's not, I'm still saving your ass."

His lips twitched, and he laid a hand gently against my cheek. "Deal. If you need me—"

"I'll send Ethan. And Rhys? If this guy shows up and he's . . . I don't know, got his claws in my power or something, get Elsmed."

"Why?"

"I don't know, but something tells me he'll know what to do."

"Were you always this bossy and interrupting?"

"Were you always this overprotective?"

"Yes," he said without pause.

I shrugged. "Guess we haven't changed then."

He grinned and pressed a quick kiss to my lips that left me panting despite the fact that it was over nearly before it began. Then he strode to the door, and with a final glance back that said everything with a single, smoldering look, he walked out.

I waited, biting my thumbnail until Rhys appeared on the lawn below. He didn't look up or acknowledge that he knew I was watching him. I hadn't expected him to. I watched in silence as he made his way around the cottages and toward the thick trees that lined the back of the property. He stopped just short of entering them, and I called to Ethan, trying to pick up on any hidden dangers he'd found.

But Ethan was quiet.

A moment later, my familiar returned, swooping low and coming to land on the railing of the balcony where I stood.

"Nothing to see out there, huh?" I asked him quietly.

Ethan offered a jerky motion that I knew was meant to be a nod.

I looked down again, but Rhys still stood at the edge of the trees, clearly debating something. Slowly, Rhys took a few steps forward until I could no longer see him from where I stood.

The moment he was out of sight, Ethan began to shriek. I gripped the railing, wondering if I should call out as well, urging Rhys back to the safety of the lawn. Too late, I realized the danger wasn't down there after all. It was here. With me.

CHAPTER 17

The door at my back creaked as it opened, and I whirled. Ethan screeched, which only added to the rush of adrenaline that poured into my veins, rooting my feet to where I stood. Deputy Conall stood in the doorway, and I didn't know whether to be relieved or terrified. Either way, my reflexes were working faster than ever. I'd already called up the magical tattoo and now held a bow in one hand and an arrow in the other. I dropped my hands to my sides at the sight of Conall.

"Gwen?" He made no move to approach me, probably because of the terror already written on my features.

I struggled to find my voice—and to make it work.

"What do you want?" I asked. The spot on my thigh where I'd inked the arrows—to hide them—still tingled from how quickly I'd spelled them into solid objects.

"We received a tip that Walter Glass has been spotted in the area. We'd like you to come down to the station until he's found."

I studied him, debating whether or not to trust him. But despite his apparent dislike for me, I had no reason to doubt his story. Doubting his identity was another matter. I kept my gaze locked on his, searching for that flash I'd seen in Dead Walter when he'd jumped from my apartment. If this was a glamour, that flash of color behind his eyes would give it away, but so far his eyes were normal.

"And Rhys?" I asked, taking a step toward him—which only made

Ethan shriek louder. "Is that what Elsmed wanted? To bring him in until this blows over?"

"Elsmed Fairchild?" Deputy Conall frowned. "Uh. I didn't realize he was involved, so I can't answer that."

I halted. "I think I'll just wait right here, if it's all the same to you."

Ethan still gave a warning sound, but the shrieking quieted.

Deputy Conall looked annoyed.

"Fine." He closed the door behind him and took up a position in the corner, leaning against the wall next to a photo print of Havenwood Falls circa fifty years ago.

"You don't have to stay," I told him.

"Actually, I do. Sheriff Kasun's orders."

I huffed.

So did he.

A moment of silence ticked by slowly.

Finally, I turned to glance back outside, scanning quickly for Rhys. He hadn't reemerged from the trees, and with every minute that he was gone, my worry grew. Something wasn't right. Not with Elsmed's cryptic summons and not with Deputy Douchebag hovering behind me.

I spun, ready to chew Conall out for whatever he'd just done. But he was still in his place in the corner.

Beside him stood Walter.

He glared at me, and I had to blink several times before I realized it wasn't my eyesight that was washing him out.

Walter was a ghost.

That was a trick I hadn't anticipated.

"Hello, Miss Facharro. It's been a while," Walter said.

Behind Walter, Deputy Conall went pale, and I could only assume being confronted with the backside of a dead guy was a first for him.

"What the hell are you doing here?" I demanded.

On the railing behind me, Ethan shrieked wildly.

"Shh," I hissed at him, so that I could hear over his shrill call.

Silent now, Ethan was practically molting. Walter watched him warily.

"I'm back to see this through," he said defiantly.

His feet never moved, but somehow he was closer now. I took a step back, wishing Rhys would hurry the hell up. Across the room, Deputy

Conall toyed with the cuffs attached to his belt. His brows were wrinkled, and I knew he was contemplating how the hell to cuff a ghost. So was I.

"See what through?" I asked.

"My deal with the Unseelie mercenary, of course." He sighed. "Trusting an Unseelie, and a Greater Fae more powerful than me, might have been my fatal mistake, but I still get my revenge . . . and I can't complain." He held up his hands and did a little dance in place. "I'm mobile again!"

I raised my brows at that. "Walter," I said, speaking as if to an ignorant child. "What the hell are you talking about?"

Walter's eyes narrowed, and his good mood vanished. "I'm talking about getting revenge on you for killing my sister."

"I didn't kill anyone."

"Maybe not directly. But your tattoos have. And that means her blood is on your hands."

My body went cold. "Your sister is . . .?"

"Sarah. My sister *was* Sarah," he corrected, "until her husband used his magical tattoo to cause her heart to fail. A tattoo that you inked and then infused with a spell. Her death is on you, and I vowed that even if it killed me, I'd see you suffer for what you'd done. It took time and a lot of planning, let me tell you, but I finally found someone who wanted you dead more than I did." He barked out a laugh. "Who knew it would be someone even more capable than me—and someone even more dangerous."

I couldn't answer, not when I could barely breathe. Walter's sister had been Sarah? The fae woman whose husband had . . .

My first magical tattoo gone awry.

I felt numb underneath the crushing weight of the familiar guilt. Aelwyn's death I could avenge. But this . . . this was justified. Whether I liked it or not, Walter was right. I deserved to suffer.

"Walter, what happened to your sister was a tragedy. I can't tell you how sorry—"

"Save it," Walter snapped. "The time for talking is over. You're my only unfinished business here, and I'd really like some god damned peace and quiet now, so just hurry up and die already."

"You're wrong," Deputy Conall said.

Walter rounded on him. "What the hell do you know about it?" he boomed.

"I know that, according to the coroner's report, iron poisoning was listed as her cause of death." Deputy Conall's voice was clear, his words certain.

I blinked.

Walter went silent.

"Are you sure?" I asked.

"Positive. I never forget a case file I sign off on."

He held my gaze, unflinching, and for the first time, his was free from annoyance.

If what he was saying was true . . .

"No, I don't believe it. Doctored the evidence. I saw the heart tattoo missing from my brother-in-law's body, and I know—"

"According to the note Lyle left, he activated that heart spell to try to save her when he'd realized what happened," Deputy Conall said.

Walter's lip curled. "Lies." He whipped around to me. "All lies to try to stop this. But it's not going to work. I will avenge Sarah."

He roared, and although I wasn't sure what he could do to me as a ghost, I backed up as he came. In a swift move, I notched the arrow in my hand and pulled it taut. When Walter still came, I let it fly.

It passed straight through Walter's ghostly form and narrowly missed Deputy Conall's shoulder as it buried itself in the wall. "Shit!" He glared at me. "Watch it."

"Sorry," I managed, but Walter was still coming.

I lowered the bow, and it clattered from my hand, useless. Damn.

Walter reached for me, and I jerked backward faster than I'd meant to when I realized his fingers had actually caught hold of my dress. They wrapped firmly around the strap and pulled. I yanked against his grip, startled. How could he touch me if I couldn't kill him? Most ghosts couldn't summon the energy necessary to manipulate the physical world, but then most ghosts weren't carrying a grudge like Walter's.

The fabric ripped away, freeing me, and I went stumbling backward onto the balcony. My heel caught on my dress, but the momentum was too strong to stop.

A sharp pain lit up my back and hips as I hit the railing. Ethan flapped his wings, desperate to move out of the way as my arms flailed. Walter still came, his ghostly eyes crazed. I felt my body give over the railing and knew I wasn't going to be able to stop myself.

I was going over.

The last thing I saw before I tumbled was another figure—ghostly and old and just as crazed as Walter, as she raced for him with her arms outstretched.

Then I fell.

I grunted, the wind whooshing out of me as two arms caught me roughly. The impact delayed the scream building in my throat, but when I opened my eyes and saw Rhys hovering over me, my relief outweighed the pain, and I sighed.

"Impeccable timing," I managed to say.

Rhys was not amused. "Are you hurt?"

I shook my head, glancing up toward the balcony. Sounds came from there—something shattering and then a moan—but I couldn't see anything. Ethan had left his perch and was circling, relieved that I was all right.

"I can walk," I said.

Rhys set me upright and held me steady until he was sure I wouldn't fall. "What happened?"

"Walter happened."

Rhys started to move, but I stopped him. "Not Walter the dark fae. Walter the ghost."

"What?"

I sighed. "It's a long story but, believe it or not, I think Madame Luiza has him under control."

Madame Luiza, Michaela's aunt who'd managed the inn for a brief time, had passed away last year. Aelwyn had spoken of rumors that she'd returned as a ghost and now spent her time watching over her family. I believed the rumors after what I'd just seen. She was not a bad security system, really.

"Luiza Petran?" Rhys asked. "Isn't she dead?"

I shrugged. "So is Walter. Sounds like a good match to me. What happened in the woods?"

He hesitated. "It was a trap."

"Where's Elsmed?"

"No idea."

"Where's your tattoo?" I asked, suddenly struck by the fact that his shirt had been peeled back to reveal smooth skin where I'd inked him last night.

"I had to use it."

"Was there something in the woods? Did you see him?"

He shook his head. "Not him. Another hellhound."

"Where would he get another hellhound?" I asked.

"No idea. I think this asshole anticipated how we would have armed ourselves and found a way to conjure his own monster to try to use up our weapons."

"But you didn't see him?" I asked, suddenly aware of how exposed we were out here.

"No. Did you?"

"I think . . . I might have."

"Where?"

"I don't know for sure but . . . follow me."

We didn't make it more than three steps before a figure appeared. Rhys and I stopped. Ethan screeched, but the figure ignored it, all his attention focused on us.

"I know who you are," I said in a voice that I hoped sounded more confident than I felt. When I'd warned Rhys earlier that the dark fae could be disguised as anyone, I hadn't realized just how true that would prove to be.

Between us and him, the darkness seemed to grow its own shadows.

The figure took a step toward us, his broad shoulders and muscled arms so familiar to me. Even the swoop of the hair over his forehead—it really had grown long—was like a comfortable blanket or the scent of herbs in the foyer at home. Something I'd know anywhere.

"Rhys," I said quietly.

Both figures answered. "Yes?"

I didn't wait for the imposter next to me to notice he'd just been outed. Instead, I rammed my elbow into his ribs and sprinted for the figure up ahead.

The real Rhys Graywalk.

CHAPTER 18

Fake Rhys roared and pushed forward, arms outstretched as he chased me. Up ahead, Real Rhys was whispering furiously at the tattoos I'd given him, willing them to form into three dimensional weapons. The knives Fake Rhys had claimed were gone suddenly sprang to life and found their way into Real Rhys's hands as he ran for us. I gathered my own magic faster than I ever had before, and the ropes I'd tattooed on my own skin sprang forth. I whispered the phrase I knew would activate the magic, nothing more than a few broken words paired with my own strength of intention, and the ropes spun out into the air, wrapping themselves almost instantly around Fake Rhys' ankles. They tightened into a lasso and then yanked hard.

He went down with a loud grunt.

Real Rhys reached me and pulled me against him in a fierce hug. He ran a hand over my hair and down my neck then pulled back long enough to search my face. "You're all right?"

"I'm good."

"How did you know it was me?" he asked while Fake Rhys thrashed on the ground nearby.

I rolled my eyes. "You weren't nearly as paranoid with worry for me as usual. And when I told you to follow me, you did it without question. That was a dead giveaway."

Real Rhys grinned and planted a hard kiss on my mouth. "Don't ever change."

It was all we had time for before Fake Rhys was groaning and pushing up on his hands. When he raised his head, his eyes were ringed in a bright yellow that was definitely not a trait he'd stolen from Rhys.

"Gwen, get back," Rhys said, already shoving me aside as he brandished his knives.

Fake Rhys was already working at untangling the ropes, but my magic held them in place. Still, it wasn't enough to stand against whatever he had. When his hands couldn't untie them, he wrapped his fingers around the rope and whispered words I didn't understand. The ropes slipped free, their spell broken.

He sprang to his feet as the ropes melted into thin air, the spellwork having run its course. Real Rhys was ready. In a move too fast for me to see, Fake Rhys drew his own set of knives, and the two men launched themselves into a violent dance accompanied by the sound of clanking metal and soft grunts.

They moved almost too fast for me to keep up with, and I knew if a human happened along, we were all going to be in a world of trouble for it. The only glamour left was the magic that held our human disguise in place. But reflexes, strength, speed, magic—it was all out there. And it was only a matter of time before the police or Elsmed or someone came along and noticed.

The longer they fought, the more I realized what an even match they were. Leaps, stabs, and parries—they moved like carbon copies of one another. Probably because they were. My anxiety left my palms clammy and Ethan practically wringing his wings in helplessness.

I had to end this. Now.

The first specks of magic on my arm sprang to life at my coaxing. Translucent images of knives and bindings, more rope like the coil I'd already unleashed and even zip ties. I kept concentrating, my impatience threatening to weaken the whole thing. But Rhys needed me, and I finally understood—and gave myself permission to use—what was really available to me. For so long, I'd held back on this part of myself, because I'd been terrified it would be used to hurt others, but I couldn't hold back anymore. It was time to use all of it.

I kept calling on the magic that was laced into the ink I wore. The weapons materialized in my hands, but it wasn't enough. Not nearly.

Before my eyes, Fake Rhys began to change form. First, his skin tone darkened until his hands and face were a darker brown than they'd been before.

While they fought, the rest of the dark fae's features changed until he no longer looked like Rhys at all. His big eyes glowed that same strange yellow as I'd seen before. His nose grew longer, and his lips thinned. His cheeks sank in, revealing a much leaner form than he'd had as Fake Rhys. His ears elongated until they came to a point, and he rose in height until he towered over the real Rhys.

I gasped as the rest of the dark fae's glamour dropped and his magic filled the air around me. It felt like invisible hands grabbing at my throat and choking me until I couldn't breathe. I coughed, then dropped to my knees as the invisible hands tightened to cut off my air completely. Dark spots danced in front of my eyes, but no matter how hard I pried, I couldn't pull the pressure away. I couldn't even get a hold on the invisible force.

Rhys heard my wheezing and turned, but the dark fae used the distraction to his advantage, and I watched in silent horror as the dark fae's knife sliced a gash in Rhys's cheek. Blood rose to the surface and then began to drip down Rhys's face.

I tried to scream but no sound came.

Rhys stumbled back, wincing and trying to regain his focus as he pressed his free hand to his cheek. The dark fae didn't chase him, and instead, he stared intently at where I knelt on the snow. His forehead creased in concentration, and I knew he was putting all his effort into attacking me now.

Desperate, I fought harder against the invisible hands at my throat, but it was no use. I waited for the moment the hands would tighten and I'd suffocate completely, but the pressure remained the same.

Slowly, my energy began to drain and my body sagged as if something or someone were siphoning my strength. One by one, the magic in the tattoos I wore began to blink out. I could feel the moment they left my body, and more than that, I could feel my own well of untapped magic growing smaller and smaller. I tried calling out to Ethan, but there was only silence where our bond had been before.

More tattoos began to appear on the dark fae, until his skin was just as covered with them as I was. Some of them glowed and some pulsed, and his eyes gleamed brighter as if the tattoos themselves were energizing him now.

Rhys roared and ran at the dark fae with his knives raised, but the dark fae parried easily and swiped the knives away. It was clear that whatever magic the dark fae was taking from me now was fueling him. If we wanted to beat him, I had to break free of his attempt to rob me of my magic

I had to take his instead.

The invisible hands around my throat remained, and the pressure was just enough to let me take small sips of air. He wanted me conscious, for now anyway. I didn't have much time, but I was determined not to let this asshole win.

My mother had said in her letter that someday they would hide from me. Today was going to be that day.

I gave up fighting against the invisible force around my throat, and instead, I put all my energy into the magic the dark fae was sucking out of me.

The magic resisted at first, and I felt like I'd been caught in a massive game of tug of war. I was sweating with the effort of calling my magic back to me, but a moment later, the pressure around my throat eased slightly. Rhys continued to circle and stab at the dark fae, and even though he wasn't making much progress with his weapons, I knew he was saving me by keeping the asshole distracted.

It was exactly what I needed now.

I kept pulling.

With a groan, I yanked one final time and took back the last of my magic. The tattoos remained on the dark fae's skin, but they no longer pulsed for him, and I knew they would answer only to me.

Using every ounce of magic I had inside me, I called out loud to the tattoos that covered the dark fae's skin. "Answer me! I am your master. Not him. Activate!"

Like I was the pied piper of ink, the tattoos peeled away from the stranger's skin and began to take form. I held my breath, hoping like hell my magic was capable of everything I suspected.

Rhys cried out, and I almost lost my hold on the magic as I jerked my attention to the two men. Both of them were winded now, their chests heaving as they stood several feet apart and eyed each other. Rhys bent over, cradling his arm. The dark fae stood tall, eyeing the injury with a look of triumph.

Fear, more real than anything I'd experienced so far, stilled me. If anything happened to Rhys . . . it wouldn't matter if I won. Not if I couldn't share the victory with him.

"Your warrior is no match for me." The dark fae sneered and then started for me.

Fear almost drowned me as I noticed how much the real Rhys was struggling to stay on his feet.

"And your magic is no match for mine," I shot back.

"My tattoos have been inked by some of the most powerful fae in the world," he said. "You are nothing compared to them. I took their power for my own, and I'll do the same to you. It is time to give your magic over to me."

The invisible hands brushed my throat again, and I scrambled back. If he was telling the truth, that meant I wasn't the first fae he'd come across with my particular gift. If he weren't trying to kill me for it, I might have been tempted to ask him about them, but those answers would have to wait.

Rhys lunged forward, knife out, distracting the dark fae once again. But I knew this burst of energy was temporary for him. If he was wounded . . . I didn't want to think about that. Or whether my preparations would be enough.

"Hang on," I called out, and then refocused everything I had back to the magic I'd called up.

Like ripping off a Band-Aid, all of the tattoos suddenly peeled away from the dark fae's skin. Not just the ones I'd felt him steal from me, but all of them. Even the ancient ink, probably from the fae he'd mentioned, ripped away from his flesh at my command.

The dark fae screamed, and I smiled grimly in satisfaction.

One by one, the tattoos floated up into the air, and then I used my magic to snuff them out. It wasn't nearly as hard as I'd imagined it to be. In fact, so much of their magic had already been poured out, they snapped like twigs against my will. When a particularly dark symbol lifted and vanished alongside the others, the dark fae stumbled. The glow in his creepy eyes dimmed.

"Whatever you're doing, keep it up," Rhys yelled.

I worked harder at snuffing out the magic of the tattoos he wore. With each one, he looked visibly weaker and slower, and I realized he stored everything in the ink. His ability to steal an appearance, the invisible hands he'd used to choke me, and finally, an intricate rune offering healing from any physical injury. Spells. They'd all been spells he'd stolen from other fae he'd hunted. One by one, I stripped them all until I could feel his magic waning.

When I got to the healing rune, I glanced over at Rhys and nodded.

"Now, Rhys," I yelled as I crushed the rune's magic with my own.

It shattered and then vanished like a dust cloud above my head.

"This is for Aelwyn," Rhys yelled, and I shivered at the depth of feeling in his words.

A second later, Rhys sent his knife flying through the air and the blade sank into the dark fae's stomach, sending the asshole to his knees.

The tendrils of invisible pressure vanished. I scrambled to my feet and rushed over to the dark fae now lying on the ground, my Rhys standing over him, his knife dripping with the fae's blood.

"Who are you?" I demanded.

He remained silent.

I crushed two more of his magical tattoos, and he winced. It gave me a sense of satisfaction to know it hurt him.

"Who are you?" I repeated.

"I am Cael, warrior for the Unseelie Court."

"You're a thief," Rhys spat as he wiped the blood from the cut on his cheek.

"You were sent by the Unseelie Court to steal my magic?" I asked.

Cael nodded, then winced, clutching at the wound on his stomach, which was bleeding a lot more heavily now than before I'd removed his healing rune.

"Why do you have tattoos?" I demanded.

"You are not the only fae who can bring their art to life," he said. "The Unseelie see the value in this gift, even if your own people do not."

"You mean you see how it can be used to hurt people," I said.

"Yes, I am aware of the Seelie's distaste for doing what must be done. It is why I am not here to recruit you."

"You act like you're doing me a favor by trying to steal my magic and then kill me," I said.

Cael sighed, but he didn't bother to argue. "We've been looking for you for a long time, but you were undetectable for years. Then Walter . . ." He broke off and started coughing.

"Walter hired you to take revenge on me because he thought I'd helped kill his sister," I finished.

Cael nodded. "His need for vengeance brought you to me on a silver platter. It also made him weak and easy to kill when it served me."

I resisted the urge to kick him for that. "But then you got a little carried away, didn't you?"

He coughed again. "Your magic is unlike anything we've ever seen. Even your mother—" He broke off, and I knelt, grabbing him by the collar. Suddenly, any hesitation I'd had over actually causing another creature harm vanished.

"What do you know about my mother?" I demanded.

"I know you're already more powerful than her if you've just destroyed my healing rune." He coughed.

Rhys looked up at me sharply, questions in his eyes, and I realized he had no idea what I'd done, because he'd been too busy fighting Cael. I ignored his confusion, my questions burning a hole right through me.

"What did you do to her?" I demanded.

"Moonlaith is well hidden. Well protected," Cael muttered, as if he hated that fact.

He blinked, and when he opened his eyes, I saw that they were no longer glowing. Probably a product of his life force draining. My shoulders sagged in quiet relief. My mother was alive. Wherever she was, she was alive.

"Her warrior was fierce," he added. "Like yours. He gave himself up to protect her and she escaped our grasp. We have not been able to get close to her since then."

In an instant, my relief vanished and was replaced by fury.

Rhys had said my mother's warrior had died protecting her, and that meant—

"You killed my father," I said through clenched teeth.

"I was following orders," Cael said, and his dismissive tone only made me angrier.

"Gwen, someone's coming," Rhys warned, and I looked up to see a couple of men approaching from across the property. They were still pretty far off, but I couldn't afford anyone to notice the amount of magic I was wielding just now. "Whatever you're going to do, do it now," Rhys added.

I didn't hesitate.

Sparks flew in more ways than one. All around me, magic snapped and crackled and left tiny sparks in its wake. Like sharpened flint grating against stone, heat surged in the air between the three of us, filling the space with electricity. My fingertips tingled even before I reached for Rhys. When my hand slid into his, my body thrummed.

One by one, Cael's tattoos shattered, and the magic was stripped from his skin. Tiny specks of light blinked on and off over our heads while I worked, and I knew it was the last of the magic snuffing out of each one of his inked spells. I could only hope those approaching were too far off to notice.

Rhys stood watching in silent wonder.

At my feet, I felt the last of Cael's life force drain away. The remnants of his tattoos and any spells inside them drained right along with his final breath. On a gasp, he shuddered and then fell still, dead.

I waited to see if any of the familiar guilt would come, but I felt only relief, and a small sense of justice. Aelwyn's killer was dead. I had killed him, but in doing so, I'd avenged both her and a father I would never meet. I was probably going to have nightmares from the entire thing, but I didn't regret what I'd done.

Beside me, Rhys squeezed my hand, and I looked up at him. His cheek was still bloody, and I remembered one last magical tattoo we still needed. With a muttering of words, the bandages on my inner wrist came to life. They took shape and dimension and then landed, wrapping around Rhys's injured arm and cheek.

He looked over at me in amusement. "Hardly important, considering."

"You are always important," I told him.

His eyes held mine, and I felt a thousand promises pass between us, unspoken. It should have felt new, this . . . thing between us. The way he rooted me to this spot with just a look and an unspoken commitment in his eyes. But it wasn't new. It had existed from the moment we'd met. The only difference between then and now was that we'd decided to acknowledge it and to let it in. We'd stopped running from it.

"It's over," I said, my voice hushed. I knew, logically, talking aloud wouldn't break the spell, because there was no spell. Not anymore. There was just us. The magic that was my love for him and his for me. But I whispered anyway.

Rhys watched me, eyes glittering. "You did it," he answered, stepping closer so that there was no more space between us.

I ran my finger over his tattoo, the still-healing lines raised into ridges on his skin. "I can't believe . . . I can't believe it's over."

"You were amazing."

I shook my head. "Not just me," I said. "You were . . . You didn't leave."

His brow shot up. "You thought I'd leave you?"

"You were supposed to get Elsmed if—"

"The only thing I'm supposed to do is kiss my girl."

"Right now? In front of all these people?" I became aware of the crowd we'd drawn, and my cheeks heated at the awareness. The figures we'd seen approaching were a few of the partygoers who had wandered far enough outside to notice the commotion we'd caused. Women in flowing gowns clutched at the arms of their dates, necks craning toward us to get a good look. No one approached, and I could only assume none of them had grown bold enough yet. But they would eventually.

"Damn straight," Rhys shot back, tightening his arm around me. "They need to know you're not available." His kiss was hard and fast and full of flourish; a message—like he'd just said.

We earned a few whistles before I pulled away, laughing softly before I could stop myself. "Show-off," I muttered.

"You just killed an Unseelie warrior without laying a finger on him, and I'm the show-off?"

"Point taken." My half-formed smile disappeared. "Oh, God. Here comes Sheriff Kasun."

Sure enough, a growling sheriff was shoving through the crowd. Deputy Conall was at his heels, still picking what looked like spider webs from his uniform.

I tensed, turning to face the sheriff so that Rhys and I stood shoulder to shoulder. Rhys squeezed my hand, but he didn't say a word as the sheriff nodded curtly at us both. His sharp blue eyes were unreadable other than the glances he threw at the cleanup crew gathering to my left. The team was a mixture of witches who I knew stood ready to investigate whether any humans had witnessed the supernatural events that had taken place here tonight. If anyone had, the witches would make sure no one remembered any of it by the time they walked away.

"Thank you all for your concern here tonight, but everything's under control," the sheriff said authoritatively. "If you'll all please step to the left and give a statement to someone from our team, we'd appreciate it. Once you're done there, you'll be free to return to the party."

The crowd took off in pairs and small groups, marching toward the team that waited for them.

When they were out of earshot, the sheriff turned back to face us, his gaze lingering on the dead man behind us. "So, either you've upped your body count, Miss Facharro, or the two of you have done me a solid and caught a killer tonight."

"Uh, definitely the second thing," I said.

"Not bad for our first date," Rhys said with a smile.

The sheriff eyed him, then me, noting our formalwear. "How romantic."

I glared at him. "You're not seriously still going to treat me like a suspect, are you?" I demanded.

"You never were a suspect, Miss Facharro. You did obstruct justice by tampering with evidence that first night, which put you at the top of my shit list for a while."

I gaped at him, but in the end, I couldn't argue with his claim. I'd definitely made a mess of that crime scene—unknowingly, but still.

"Sorry," I mumbled.

"I thought you said—" Rhys began with a frown.

"Son, I think it's time we had a talk about your access to confidential case information where Miss Facharro's concerned," Sherriff Kasun interrupted.

"I'm authorized, as her Protector, to—"

"You're a lot more than that, though, aren't you?" Sherriff Kasun gave him a look and he looked back at me, a soft smile playing on his lips.

"Yes, sir," he said quietly.

"Precisely. Anyway, I've got a team on the way to process the body you've brought me tonight," the sheriff went on. "And I suspect the energy signature will match the unauthorized portal entry from a while back. While we wait, why don't you tell me what happened here tonight."

"Sir, you're also going to want to send a team upstairs," Deputy Conall said.

Sheriff Kasun followed Conall's glance up to the balcony I'd fallen from earlier. "We got another body up there?"

"Not a body per se," Deputy Conall said slowly.

"What the hell is it?" Sheriff Kasun demanded.

"A ghost," Deputy Conall said on a sigh. "He'll need to be charged with conspiracy to commit murder—among other things."

"A . . .?" Sheriff Kasun stared at him and then finally drew a long breath, shaking his head. "Can we ever have a normal night? All right. Call in a second team."

Deputy Conall nodded and hurried off, pulling his phone out.

At the same moment, Elsmed appeared, clearly rattled. "Well?" he demanded.

"What?" Sheriff Kasun frowned.

"Is someone here going to tell me why I received a note from a salty vampire to meet you all at the tattoo shop when you're all clearly still here?"

Sheriff Kasun pinned me with a look. "You. Tragic Ink. Start talking."

CHAPTER 19

Snug and warm in my thick coat and wool gloves, I adjusted my pack, slowing to navigate a stream that had frozen over months back. The only sound our party made now was the crunch of our boots. Up ahead, Rhys cut a path as straight as he could, considering there was no real trail to our destination, not in the snow anyway. I couldn't believe I was leaving this winter wonderland behind. I'd never been beyond the town limits, and here I was leaving this realm altogether. At least it hadn't required a passport. I almost snorted at that, because it had been nearly as complicated working out our travel details as a rushed passport would have been.

Behind me, Elsmed muttered words that sounded like crooning compliments. Ethan perched on his shoulder, his beady, black eyes constantly scanning. I still couldn't understand what drew him to Elsmed of all people; I could barely get him to sit like that for me. I wondered if it had something to do with Elsmed's telepathic abilities.

Rhys stopped and waited for the rest of us to catch up.

I hurried forward, excited—and more than a little nervous—to get a look at the portal.

"Um, am I missing something?" I asked, turning a complete three-sixty before frowning. "There's nothing here but a bunch of rocks."

Rhys raised a brow. "Be patient. We have to activate it first. It's not like we can leave the door open all the time. Any sort of creature could slip right in."

I gave him a look.

"Again," he added ruefully.

I shook my head.

Cael's body had been transported and sent through the portal a few days back. A different portal than the one we were using now. I was more than okay with that. Sharing my arrival into the faerie realm with a dead criminal wasn't exactly my ideal impression.

"Right, makes sense." I took a deep breath to steady my nerves.

Rhys grabbed my elbow and bent closer, lowering his voice even though Elsmed was still a ways off. "You don't need to be nervous," Rhys said. "She already loves you."

"I know. I just . . . It's a lot."

He nodded. "I can imagine." Then he put his arms around me and pulled me close, propping his chin on my head while he held me. "But we both know it's not nearly as heavy as that misplaced guilt you've been carrying around."

"True." It was a huge relief to know my tattoo hadn't killed Walter's sister. My magical tats were still capable of a lot of damage. The hellhound was proof of that, and I still battled with that guilt a bit. But learning the truth about Sarah had made me realize everyone was responsible for their own actions. My tattoos could be used for good—or for evil. It wasn't up to me once the ink had dried.

Rhys seemed more relieved than I was to hear I'd let some of that shit go. It had also allowed us to reconnect, catching up on the years we'd been apart. Standing here in the circle of his arms made me think of some of those reconnections now. I was snug and warm like this, and I almost didn't want to let go, but we had a portal to catch.

Elsmed joined us, still chatting to Ethan. He looked at us expectantly as he came close. "Well?" he asked. "Are you both ready then?"

I shot a glance at Rhys. "I think so."

"Good. Now remember, once you're settled, the Seelie Court would like to meet you both. Rhys will need to make a statement about his mission here, and I suspect they'll want to get to know you, too, Gwen. If you want help setting that up, get in contact with Chase MacElvoy."

"Who is he?" I asked.

"Chase is our Seelie representative. He travels back and forth from here to Tír na nÓg regularly, so he can help coordinate your appearance with the Court there."

"Tír na nÓg?" I repeated, trying to place the name from everything I'd heard of the Seelie Court.

"It's a small island off the coast, and it's the capital of the Seelie Court. Chase has an office there, so just contact him when you're ready, and he can bring you home. But take your time." His gaze settled on me. "When you return or how long you stay is completely up to you. Just remember —time passes differently in Faerie. A couple of weeks could equal months here."

"Thank you," I told him, startled to realize how far we'd come in a short time. Elsmed had been completely terrifying to me when we'd first met—what? Two weeks ago? And now, at least to me anyway, he was one of the friendliest faces in this town. Not that any of the others were unfriendly. Not anymore.

"You're welcome. As for your personal affairs while you're gone . . ." Elsmed said the words like a question.

Rhys jumped in. "Everything's in order, sir. My bar manager is in charge with complete autonomy while I'm gone. Gwen's shop is closed until further notice."

"I'm told Aelwyn's house belongs to both of you now," Elsmed said.

We both nodded. We'd been over this with Sheriff Kasun and a lawyer during the past week. The sheriff had been a lot friendlier after we'd caught Cael for him—a strike against him that meant I probably wouldn't be sending him a Christmas card anytime soon. But at least I wasn't on his short list of "chicks capable of murder" anymore. Deputy Conall had actually hugged me when I'd given my statement. *Weirdo.*

I planned to resume my mistletoe supplements the moment we stepped foot back in Havenwood Falls.

Thanks to Aelwyn's savvy financial foresight, the taxes and mortgage were both paid for the next few years. Which meant we were keeping the house until after our trip. I didn't want to think about it right now, but I'd probably never sell it. It was home in a way Faerie could never be. Rhys agreed.

"All right, I think that's everything. Oh," Elsmed held his arm out. "You'll want him back I suppose."

I returned Ethan safely back to my skin, and then Elsmed surprised me by offering his gloved hand for a shake. A handshake wasn't all that foreign, but I'd never really seen him touch anyone before. Another thing

I could blame on the mistletoe. Maybe this was what it felt like to be normal?

I shook and gave him a smile. "Thank you for arranging all this," I told him earnestly.

"It's the least I could do." He bent lower, his voice dropping as if he were sharing private information. "Speaking of arrangements, I wanted to let you know that there are . . . circumstances at work regarding your blackmailing problem. I think, by the time you return, that particular problem will have worked itself out."

I blinked. "Wow. Thank you so much."

Elsmed's eyes seemed to twinkle, and then he moved on to Rhys. "Son." They shook stiffly. "You don't need me to tell you, but keep our girl safe, will you? Bring her back."

"Will do."

Rhys was so solemn, their handshake so formal, I rolled my eyes.

But then Elsmed stepped back. He closed his eyes and murmured words in a language I'd never heard before. A moment later, the rock façade that loomed before me began to move. Small ripples started in the center and ringed outward, like the surface of a lake after throwing a rock into it.

I watched in awe as the ripples spread and the liquid grew lighter—until I wasn't looking at a surface so much as seeing through it.

Rhys slid his hand into mine and squeezed.

My stomach tightened with nerves again as a figure came into view on the other side. A woman, tall and slender with flowing hair, stood just beyond the veil.

"Is that—?"

"Moonlaith," Elsmed said from behind me. "Sure looks like. Give her my regards, would you?"

I didn't answer. I couldn't speak around the lump in my throat. My hands were clammy inside my gloves.

Rhys looked over at me. "Are you ready?"

I nodded, knowing full well I wasn't ready. How could anyone ever be ready for something they were positive would never happen? My whole life, I'd believed my mother was dead. Never coming back. Gone. And now, here she was, standing just on the other side of this portal. A few steps away.

Hell no, I wasn't ready for that.

But I also wasn't going to stand still any longer. I was going to live my life moving forward. No more hiding what I was and what I could do.

With feet that felt like lead, I took one step. Then another. With each footfall, they became easier. Until I was passing through the strange gel of the portal and through the magic to the other side. The woman waiting smiled at me, her hair white like the moon. Her smile soft and warm. Like a mother's. I kept walking—straight into her open arms. And I knew I'd always look back on this moment and think, *This is when it all began.*

WE HOPE you enjoyed this story in the Havenwood Falls series featuring a variety of supernatural creatures. The series is a collaborative effort by multiple authors.

Books in the main Havenwood Falls series:

Forget You Not by Kristie Cook
Old Wounds by Susan Burdorf
Fate, Love & Loyalty by E.J. Fechenda
Covetousness by Randi Cooley Wilson
The Winged & the Wicked by T.V. Hahn & Kristie Cook
Alpha's Queen by Lila Felix
Ink & Fire by R.K. Ryals
Lose You Not by Kristie Cook
Tragic Ink by Heather Hildenbrand
Nowhere to Hide by Belinda Boring
Flames Among the Frost by Amy Hale (April 2018)
Rock Me Gently by Susan Burdorf (May 2018)

More books releasing on a monthly basis

Also try the YA line, Havenwood Falls High.

Subscribe to our reader group and receive free stories and more!

IMMERSE yourself in the world of Havenwood Falls and stay up to date on news and announcements at www.HavenwoodFalls.com. Join our reader group, Havenwood Falls Book Club, on Facebook at https://www.facebook.com/groups/HavenwoodFallsBookClub/

ABOUT THE AUTHOR

Heather Hildenbrand was born and raised in a small town in northern Virginia, where she was homeschooled through high school. (She's only slightly socially awkward as a result.) She writes paranormal and contemporary romance with plenty of abs and angst. Her most frequent hobbies are riding motorcycles and avoiding killer slugs.

You can find out more about Heather and her books at heatherhildenbrand.com or sign up for email updates.

ACKNOWLEDGMENTS

First, I have to say a big thank you to Kristie for inviting me into the world of Havenwood Falls. I am so honored to be a part of something so unique and alive! Thanks to the entire team at Ang'dora. It's because of you, this story actually shines! Special thanks to Randi Cooley Wilson, Kallie Ross, and E.J. Fechenda for helping me include some of their characters in these pages. It's such a cool thing to be able to share in this way—also, I'm a huge Everett fan so I am kind of swooning that I got to write him into a few corners of my own story. (If you haven't read *Covetousness* by Randi Cooley Wilson, what are you even doing with your life?)

To my early—and emergency—beta readers: Amber Shepherd and Rebecca Pruner Kimmel, you guys made this story WAY better, and I am so lucky that you're always willing to read my stories on short notice. I still have no idea how you are able to do that. I swear, it's like a superpower.

And to my readers, my Love Birds, thank you guys for always reading with such excitement! Your ideas helped shape this story early on, and I can always count on our Facebook tribe to help me out when I get stuck. I appreciate all of you! See you in the next book!

~ A Havenwood Falls New Adult Novella ~

HAVENWOOD FALLS

NOWHERE TO HIDE

BELINDA BORING

AN EXCERPT

Nowhere to Hide (A Havenwood Falls Novella) by Belinda Boring

Fact One: A flock of crows is called a murder.

Fact Two: Cherophobia is the fear of fun.

Fact Three: It's impossible to sneeze with your eyes open.

For Sedona Mathews, facts and knowledge act as a buffer between her and the outside world. Born as an empath, others' emotions bombard her senses, complicating any relationship she's tried to enjoy. When she becomes sole owner of Shelf Indulgence, she happily devotes her life to the Havenwood Falls bookstore, hiding away amongst books she loves. Because there's another fact Sedona is painfully aware of . . .

Fact Four: In a town where nothing and no one is as they seem, falling in love can be treacherous.

Micah Westbrook has no time for love. Cloaked in secrecy, he brings his niece, Holly, to Havenwood Falls, hoping they can hide amongst the other supernaturals. He's charged with keeping Holly safe and will risk everything to ensure those hunting them can't pick up their trail. The last thing Micah needs is to be blindsided by a danger he didn't see coming . . . Sedona.

Micah struggles to keep her at arm's length, forgetting one important fact: When it comes to loving an empath, there's nowhere to hide.

NOWHERE TO HIDE

AN EXCERPT

*Y*ou *can do it, Sedona. There's no need to panic. Everything will be okay. Just put on your big girl panties, smile, and pretend that you can't feel everything he is thinking.*

If I had a dollar for every time I'd rehearsed this small mantra, standing here at the window of my bookstore, Shelf Indulgence, I'd have enough to leave Havenwood Falls and explore the world for the rest of my life.

Not that I truly wanted to leave the only place I'd ever felt safe enough to call my home, but you get the idea.

I sounded like a broken record that kept skipping and repeating the same old tired words. Part of me wished I could toss aside my reservations each time I decided to bravely face the possibilities of dating.

The problem was there was nothing normal about beginning a new relationship, especially when you held the special gifts I did. My mother used to tell me how unique being an empath was, and that when my ability was paired together with my other inherent powers, I would become a force to be reckoned with.

Those pep talks ended by the time I reached my teens, replaced by the now familiar fear that echoed in her heart. She was careful to prevent it from ever shining out through her eyes or filling her voice when she spoke. I didn't need those nonverbal cues to know what she was feeling.

The empathy I'd been raised to believe was a gift morphed quickly into a curse—one that kept my peers at arm's length, their soft whispers following behind me as I walked down Havenwood Falls High's hallways. I didn't blame them for not wanting to invite me to sit with them at lunch or bond over fun sleepovers.

Even though many of them were part of the hidden supernatural community, somehow their fangs, claws, and weirdness weren't nearly as dangerous as being able to reach into them and pluck out their secret feelings.

It wasn't until I found comfort in running Shelf Indulgence and escaping into the beloved books I cherished that I made my peace with who I was—am.

"I could always cancel," I murmured, my stomach churning with nerves. "It's only a first date . . . nothing important." My throat dried the second I spotted Robert crossing the street, headed in my direction. "God, I hate this."

A deep, familiar voice answered. "One of us needs to leave this store and have a life, Sedona. And considering I can't, that leaves the burden firmly on your shoulders."

Maxwell appeared beside me, his fingers twirling the end of his mustache. I often wondered if he realized he did that—if it was a nervous habit he'd failed to break. I couldn't quite cross out an alternative thought that it was his way of impersonating a villain because right now, my dearest friend wasn't enabling my cowardice at all. He was supposed to agree wholeheartedly with me and suggest I spend the evening secluded quietly in my apartment with a delicious glass of wine and a book.

"I still think you made that up, Maxwell. I'm sure if you tried hard enough, you could leave and go haunt Willow over at Coffee Haven. You know . . . expand your horizons and all."

A look of horror and disapproval blazed across his ghostly features.

Did I forget to mention Maxwell was a ghost?

"I'll pretend I didn't hear you suggest that, young lady. Do you really think I'd stay here and witness your weekly neurotic diatribe about the woes of dating if I could simply waltz out of here?"

I knew Maxwell well enough to remember that beneath his offended pout, he was teasing me. Like he said, we pretty much went through this conversation each time I foolishly agreed to go out with someone. We both had our parts to play.

Clenching my hands into fists, I straightened and drew in a deep breath. "How do I look? Am I presentable enough?"

Despite my blasé attitude toward dating, I still found myself making an effort, a small sliver of hope surfacing that maybe, just maybe, this time would be different.

"You look beautiful as always. Although," he paused for a moment, casting a glance outside as Robert drew closer. The corners of his lips twitched into an almost smile. In stepping off the curb, my date had misjudged the slickness of the ground, his feet slipping over ice. To some, winter in Havenwood Falls was far from the magical wonderland that I viewed it as. Robert's mouth formed a silent curse word.

Maxwell cleared his throat, bringing my attention back to our conversation. "I believe your beauty is wasted on this human."

There was no mistaking the sneer in his tone. My dear friend didn't approve of my dating someone outside our supernatural community.

"You know why I agreed," I retorted, steeling myself to once again remind him that there were slim pickings for me no matter how hard I tried.

Who would want to date an empath?

"Heathens," Maxwell exhaled in disgust. "In my day, men would be lining up around the town square for a chance to be with you."

"Well, pity we can't just hop in a time machine and find me these rare males." I laughed, desperately hoping it disguised the sadness I couldn't always bury. Truth be told, I was lonely. Just once, I wanted to experience the toe-curling, heart-racing, giddy swooning love I read about.

My gaze remained with Robert now—the moment I'd been waiting for. The closer he came, the sooner I would sense his intentions. Over the years, I'd become pretty good at protecting myself from the overwhelming crush of emotions that surrounded me. It was one of the first spells I perfected when I came of age and could practice magic on my own. Invisible to the naked eye, a silvery aura encased me, thinning only when I purposely lowered my guard to get a reading of someone.

He must've sensed I was watching because a huge smile lit his face when our eyes met. Everything seemed normal as his intentions mentally reached me—nerves over whether he could impress me, a list of topics to cover over dinner just in case we ran out of things to say, and that he believed I was one of the prettiest girls he'd ever laid eyes on.

That last one made my own smile grow. What girl didn't like knowing others thought she was attractive?

Robert was only a few steps away from the store's door when I caught the briefest of flashes of another feeling—one that instantly brought the shutters around my heart. Sighing sadly, I knew I couldn't forget and pretend he hadn't just cast aside those other emotions for one that made my skin crawl.

Lust. The lewd kind that left you feeling stripped bare and vulnerable in front of a group of men catcalling and yelling for you to shake what the good lord gave you.

I was far from being a prude, so lust in general wasn't something to make me retreat. There was nothing wrong with finding someone good-looking and noticing how they made your body respond.

That wasn't how Robert was feeling right now. If anything, he was contemplating how long it would take him to get me flat on my back, legs in the air, as I screamed his name in worship.

"Blech," I uttered, already heading to the door. "Be right back, Maxwell." Not giving him a chance to reply, to convince me I didn't have the luxury of turning yet another man down, or to list the million reasons he worried I would become the Cat Lady of Havenwood Falls, I was out on the street. I was the queen of excuses, and I didn't feel guilty for the lies I told Robert, or the fake disappointment I expressed over having to cancel the plans he had for us.

It took everything I had not to shudder when he rubbed my arm, his touch lingering longer than was appropriate. Another blast of lust shot out from him, and I took a few steps backward.

I couldn't run back inside the bookstore fast enough, leaving Robert standing on the sidewalk, confused over how I could possibly choose something over him. His arrogance was another turnoff—something he'd managed to hide when he'd asked me out earlier in the week.

"What was the reason this time?" Maxwell asked, exasperated. If he rolled his eyes any harder, they would've fallen to the back of his head and down his body, before coming to a stop in his feet. Snarky ghost.

"Unexpected inventory audit," I answered weakly. Even I could hear what a lousy reason it was. "In my defense, he was a pig."

His brows furrowed in concern. "You can't keep doing this, Sedona. Do you honestly want to end up like me?"

"I could think of worse things to become." In trying to lighten the conversation and perhaps deflect the lecture I sensed brewing within him, I couldn't deny he had a point. "Next time I'll go, okay? Just not with him."

He snorted. "What was wrong with this one?"

My face flushed. "Let's just say, if given the chance, he'd rather have skipped dinner and dived right into dessert."

A deep baritone laugh burst from Maxwell. "He found you attractive and that upset you? You do know what happens when two people like each other, Sedona? Please tell me I don't have to inform you about the birds and the bees."

The very thought made me squirm uncomfortably. "I already know about sex, smart-ass." I shook my head at him. "I just don't like it when the guy I'm with is more interested in getting between my legs than really getting to know me."

"And here I thought I was the old-fashioned one," he retorted quickly. "You can't hide away in here forever, Sedona. Sexual sparks are a good thing. You need chemistry." His voice grew louder and more passionate. "The heroes in those romance books you love won't keep you warm at night. You need someone real."

"Says the ghost that won't leave either." It was a low blow, but I was feeling defensive.

In the years since I'd taken over my grandfather's bookstore and made it my own, I'd never once seen Maxwell leave. He'd simply appeared one day, and no amount of questioning would get him to reveal where he'd come from.

"My circumstances are different." His response was gruff. As an empath, I couldn't get a fix on his emotions, my gifts reserved solely for the living, but in this case, I didn't need to rely on my gift to know what he was feeling.

We were both defensive.

"I'll try harder next time," I promised, wishing I could reach out and touch him without my hand passing through. "He just wasn't right for me."

"You can't afford to be so selective. You need to seize the moment before time slips through your fingers. Take it from me." His voice trailed off.

It was on the tip of my tongue to ask him why, to perhaps prod a little to see if he would finally open up and share.

I didn't get the chance, however, as the door to the store opened, startling me. Maxwell disappeared, leaving me standing there like a fool, talking to myself. Most times that wouldn't bother me. Most of the town believed I was weird anyway, so nothing really surprised them.

As my heart began racing and my mouth instantly dried, all I could think was two things:

One, I hoped this guy didn't think I was a freak too.

Two, the stranger standing in the doorway, his gorgeous blue eyes fixed completely on me, was by far the sexiest man I had ever seen.

And when he spoke, I knew I was in trouble.

Find *Nowhere to Hide* at your favorite book retailer.

www.ingramcontent.com/pod-product-compliance
Lightning Source LLC
Chambersburg PA
CBHW051949170626
46808CB00007B/2537